PEN AMERICA BEST DEBUT SHORT STORIES 2017

PEN AMERICA BEST DEBUT SHORT STORIES 2017

EDITOR'S NOTE

Emily Chammah's "Tell Me, Please" is a love story that is a triumph of subtlety. All the concentrated yearning of adolescence is contained in these pages, provoked by everyday events and conversation. Amal, the younger daughter in a traditional Arabic family living on the outskirts of Amman, Jordan, reminds us how intensely we observe our families to learn how to live, and how painful it can be to desire to break from expectations. Amal's increasingly complicated understanding of intimacy with her cousin Omar is woven against the warm backdrop of a loving family, and these pressures, from without and within, crystallize in piercing hopes and disappointments. Chammah's language is rich, detailed, elegant, and specific; not for a moment do we forget whose mind and heart we are embodying. It was a privilege to encounter this story again and again through the editing process, and to publish it for others to dwell in Amal's world and relish all of its keen sensation and life.

Jennifer Acker, editor in chief
The Common

TELL ME, PLEASE

Emily Chammah

I WOULDN'T SAY that Omar is my best friend, because I like to think we are closer than that, that there is something bringing us together more than any friendship could. While it is true that he is my cousin, I never feel as connected to the others—to Muhammad or Nour or Ahmed or Anais—or even to my older sister, Sousan. They don't know, for example, that I prefer to drink my orange juice without sugar, that I'd rather eat falafels straight out of a paper cone than smashed inside a pocket of bread.

Omar's mother and mine are sisters, and every afternoon before our fathers come home from work, they visit in the family's sitting room with sugary tea and cigarettes. Omar and I sit on the carpeted floor at their feet. We draw pictures of pigeons and kites, or turn the pages of my father's atlas, making up stories about the kinds of people who live in Greece and Turkey and Japan. For us, everyone is like our parents, drinking thick cups of coffee and praying five times a day. The differences between one people and another are often small and silly—Omar once said that children in Japan wear only yellow shoes and orange socks, and I once said that the women in Greece wear crowns of leaves on top of their hijabs. We roll on the carpet and laugh until our mothers tell us to hush, sending us to the roof, where we try to smoke the cigarettes we've pinched from their purses and practice calling our own azans.

Omar and I write each other notes in English, a language our parents cannot read. The letters are too rigid, too angled for them to see properly. My mother doesn't know the difference between *l*'s and *i*'s, and though my father knows a handful of words—*hello, thank you, no, yes*—he hasn't tried to sound out letters on a page since he was in school many years ago.

Which is lucky for Omar and me. We can tell stories and share secrets and dreams without the risk of being found out. But our English is weak, we do not know as many words as we do in Arabic, and, because of it, our secrets aren't really secrets at all.

Hello, sir! My name is Amal. What is your name? I once wrote.

Or, *Jordan: The Diamond in the Desert*, which is something I saw the only time my mother and father took me to Amman. We had visited the Citadel and the Roman Theatre and sipped cups of lentil soup from a cart. As we walked back to the bus station, we passed a travel agency whose posters and signs were in English, and I saw the beautiful description written on a postcard. How true, I thought to myself, though when I tugged on the fabric of my mother's dress to show her, a taxi hit a man crossing the road, and everyone's attention turned to the old man, his body still, and the driver, standing nearby, holding his head between his hands. A crowd began to form, and a young man selling newspapers covered the body with the day's news, with King Abdullah waving to all of us from the front page. Now, whenever I bring up that day, my mother shakes her head and says, I swear to God I will never go back to Amman.

✦

ONCE, OMAR WROTE, *My mother has green eyes and I have brown eyes.* But my eyes are brown, not his. His are the color of honey, liquid and warm like molten gold.

Another time: *My name is Omar. It is nice to meet you, Miss Amal.* This note I keep under my pillow, though sometimes, after Sousan turns out the lights, I like to unfold the square of paper— now soft from all of my handling—and hide it under my pajama top, next to my skin.

Eventually, Omar and I stop spending our afternoons together. We no longer take the long route to the market where we buy mint for our mothers' tea; we no longer whisper into each other's ears stories about people from faraway lands.

It is indecent, my mother says. What will the others think?

I say, They will think that we are cousins, that we are friends!

Heat radiates from my cheeks.

No, habibiti, she says, shaking her head. No, they will not. You are a woman now, and he is becoming a man. It isn't proper for you to be alone with him.

But, Mamma, I—

I don't finish my sentence, because my chest is pounding and my face is wet.

Sousan adjusts the hijab she's just wrapped around my head. She curls her arms around my waist, rests her chin on my shoulder. Don't worry, Amal. You're one of us now. He's just a silly boy.

That's not true! I say, and storm into the bathroom, locking the door behind me. I stare into the mirror, into my own eyes, bloodshot from the tears. My lips are swollen, my stomach churning. Sousan and my mother knock on the door, try to coo me out, but eventually let me be.

✦

How strange it is to rethink your understanding of a person overnight. How strange it is to go to bed a girl, and wake up a woman. How strange it is to feel like everyone around you knows your secrets.

Oh, Amal, what is it you hope for?
Where, in the whole wide world, would you like to go?
What do you think of when you are alone?
These are the kinds of things I wish Omar would have asked me.

Omar grows, and so do I.

I no longer know, for example, if he plays soccer in the street. I do not know if he prefers meat over chicken, his coffee sweetened or plain. I do not know if he remembers our stories about people in foreign lands, if he looks back on those orange afternoons with the same fondness I do.

I'm not going to say my decision to study English was purely motivated by Omar. It wasn't, of course. But I will say there was a time when English felt like a secret, a sacred thing only we shared. I will say there was a time when I thought that if I were to study as best as I could, if I were able to speak and write clearly and beautifully in this language so different from my own, that no matter how much we would change or grow apart, Omar and I would still be connected.

Omar's mother and mine continue to visit every afternoon. I still join them on the carpet, though now I'm the one to make the tea—with sprigs of mint in the summer and velvety ears of sage in the winter. Now, I don't hide the fact that I know how to hold a cigarette, that I am able to pull a column of smoke through my teeth without coughing.

Where did she learn this? Aunt Hanan asks. She is clever, this one.

I blush, and return to my book.

Is it possible she tells Omar this about me? That I continue to sit at her and my mother's feet, though instead of reading my father's atlas, I read Dickens and Wilde and Woolf?

Yes, she is clever. But don't tell her father about the cigarettes, my mother says.

Or the books.

Aunt Hanan laughs, and so do I.

My father isn't opposed to my reading; no, not at all. It is more that he doesn't like me to read something he cannot himself. So, he insists that for every book I bring home, I also find a translation in Arabic, one that he can skim or read along, if he'd like. (Though he doesn't often like.)

One afternoon, Aunt Hanan walks in overflowing with joy, carrying plates of kunafe and flaky pastries soaked in rosewater.

Omar, she explains, has been given a scholarship to study at the University of Jordan. He is going to study medicine, become a doctor.

We all embrace and sing praises of Omar. Omar, the one with perfect marks, the one with the kind soul, the one with honey eyes.

But where will he live? my mother asks. Not in Mafrag?

My heart falls into my stomach.

What is it, my dear Amal, that you want?

No, no, of course not, Aunt Hanan goes on. They will pay for a dormitory in Amman.

My mother shakes her head. Inshallah he will be safe in that city, she says.

✦

BEFORE SOUSAN IS married and moves to the other side of town, she and Ahmed are able to visit once a week for thirty minutes, alone.

He brings her chocolates.

He brings her small teddy bears.

He stands nervously in the guest sitting room, waiting.

My mother watches when they first greet. They shake hands, lean their bodies close to each other. He hands her flowers, she beams. My mother, holding a wooden spoon, pats me on the small of my back.

Let them be alone, she tells me, nodding toward the door that separates the guest space from our family's. But be sure to listen.

She turns off the television and returns to the kitchen, where she prepares a tray of snacks and juice.

The thing about Sousan having time alone with her fiancé is this: While they could be kissing or touching, at any moment, any-one—me or my mother—could enter through the sliding door. And, since the front door does not lead to the family's quarters but to the guests', my father, scheduled to arrive home any time now, could walk in.

And, if he caught them embracing in any way, it could mean that the wedding would be off, that ties would be severed between the families, that a war might ignite within the clan.

No wonder Ahmed is nervous.

I tell my mother that I'll keep my ears open, but, to be honest, it doesn't matter much to me. They'll be married soon enough, and when we slide the door closed and my mother retreats into the back of the house, all I can think about is the thirty minutes I will have, alone, on the computer.

Both Sousan and I have Facebook accounts, though we've had to skew our names so that our identities remain secret. Nowhere on our pages can you find real information about us—the fact that we are sisters, that we are from the Beni Hasan tribe, that we live in Mafrag, that we attend Al al-Bayt University.

Which makes searching for us—or for any of our friends, for that matter—impossible.

Sousan is Sou Sou Jordan (in Arabic letters), and I'm Amëlië Hopë (in English).

Her profile pic is a drawing: an anime-style girl with large brown eyes and a lime-green hijab. Mine is a sunset on a beach, with the words *Waking up to see another day is a blessing. Don't take it for granted. Make it count and be happy that you're alive.*

Though we change them regularly.

About a month ago, I found Omar's page. Omar Khaled (in both Arabic and English), the University of Jordan. He doesn't have to act with such secrecy, though he doesn't post much about himself (what he thinks of Amman, if he misses the quiet of Mafrag, etc.).

The day I found his name, my heart seemed to want to beat out of my chest.

I added him, and sent a message in English: Ya, 3mar, I am your cousin, Amal. We miss you here in Mafrag!

He sent one back: Hi, my cousin Amal! It is good to hear from you. How is Mafrag?

I said: 7mdullah, 7mdullah.

And that was the end of our conversation.

I wondered whether or not I should have asked him about life in Amman, if I should have been the one to open the doors of communication so that we might write to each other once again. I was nervous, but why should I have been? He is Omar, my closest and one true friend.

Now I have taken to looking at his page, to clicking through his profile pics, waiting for each to load, row by row of tiny little pixels, one at a time.

Omar has sixty-seven pictures. Because our connection is slow, in the thirty minutes I have alone, I've only seen nine.

A member of the Barcelona football team whooping in celebration.

The University of Jordan medical school.

A sun setting behind a minaret.

Prince William and Prince Harry, arms thrown around each other.

A black-and-white photograph of a little boy kicking a soccer ball down an empty street.

The Jordanian flag.

Omar in front of the gates of the university, wearing sunglasses and making a backwards peace sign.

A Barcelona football jersey.

Omar in a red keffiyeh. (This is my favorite, and I linger on it for a few moments until I click to the next picture, which may be why I have only seen a fraction of them.)

Today, I take in a deep breath at the sight of his golden eyes against the red-and-white fabric, and click on.

A platter of mansef.

The Jordanian flag again.

The next takes longer to load than the rest.

From the first little bit that appears, I can tell that this picture was not taken with a phone or found on a website. This picture is old, a photograph that has been scanned onto a computer.

I dig my toes into the carpet and think, Why does that tawny background look so familiar?

At the next pixelated line, I notice white fringe, what looks like a moon of shiny black hair rising out of the blank space.

Off in the kitchen, my mother calls my name. Ya, Amal! You still listening?

I turn my head to call to her—Yes, Mamma, everything's okay!—and notice the white fringe of our hand-woven rug, the caramel carpet of our sitting room. Could this photograph have been taken here?

When I look back at the computer, I begin to see Omar's head, his bright eyes pinching at the corners, his mouth smiling plenty. Next to him seems to be a little girl: me.

My breathing quickens, my knee bounces up and down. While I often grow impatient waiting for Omar's profile pics to load, nothing compares to this stress welling up inside of me.

Ya, Amal! They have three more minutes. In three minutes, open the door.

Three minutes, three minutes. Is that long enough to load the photograph? I am praying that it is.

Ya, Amal, come and help me gather plates and spoons.

I hesitate, not wanting to leave the computer. I never leave Facebook open, for fear that my parents might look through my messages or posts. And I'd never leave it open on the page of a boy. But this photograph is taking what feels like forever, and so I rush to the kitchen, scramble to grab the tiny plates and spoons as quickly as possible and bring them to the sitting room.

Slow down, girl—there's no rush! my mother says.

I nod and, with the plates stacked upon a copper tray, head back to the computer.

There, on the screen, is a picture of Omar and me, him in a brown shirt, me in a yellow sweater. We're about ten years old, sitting on this exact carpet that I rub with my feet, thumbing through my father's atlas. His eyes look at the camera, but mine look at him, our smiles missing teeth.

Dozens of comments in both Arabic and English drag along the side of the page.

CuTe CuTe. <3 :)

Awww, she loves youuuuuu.

3mar, you were so sweet.......what happened? :p

ما شاء الله

7elwa kiteeeeeeeeeeeeeeeeer!!!!!!!!!!!!!!!!!!!!

My mother yells from the kitchen. Amal! Tell them their time is up!

She slowly proceeds into the sitting room, balancing a carafe of coffee, bowls of sugar, and demitasse cups in her hands.

I don't want to leave this photograph, this memory, this pure, childish happiness, but I don't want my mother to see. I quickly like the picture, close the browser, and slide open the door to Sousan and Ahmed.

Alarmed by my force, they jump away from each other on the couch and stand, their faces red.

Excuse me, I say. Coffee.

Oh, Amal, do you ever think of me?
Dear Amal, who is your closest friend?
Tell me: What in the world would you like to see?

✦

THE NEXT WEEK, when Sousan and Ahmed visit behind the sliding door, I log on to Facebook.

I have thirty notifications, mostly friends of Omar commenting on the picture that I've now brought to the surface of his News Feed.

Oh, sweeeeeeeeet!!! Who is this little girl?

Mosta7eel! This innocent face couldn't possibly be you.

No it's him! He's such a mamma's boy.

Omar, oh, Omar. You were a ladies' man even back then!

This last post unsettles me. Does Omar have girlfriends in Amman? Are they foreign students, from America or Europe? Does he go to swanky cafés with velvet cushions and milk shakes, to smoke lemon-and-mint flavored argeela? Has he ever held a girl's hand, or kissed one on the cheek?

Oh, Omar, what is your life like in the city?

He responds to these comments like this:

hhhhhhhhhh merci, merci. this is me and my favorite cousin when we were very young and adorable.

Omar, I am sure that you are still adorable.

I have five messages: two from my friend Aliya, one from my cousin Nour, one from Sousan, and one from Omar.

And, upon seeing this, I find that it has become difficult to breathe.

I open the message, which he has composed in formal Arabic.

Dearest Amal,

I saw that you "liked" the photograph of us as children.
I hope that posting the picture was not a problem . . .
it is one of many photographs I brought to Amman to
remind me of home, and one afternoon when I was

studying for exams and feeling quite lonely, I scanned it at the library and made it my profile picture.

I am sorry if the comments my friends have written embarrassed or offended you. If you would prefer, I can delete it.

Sincerely,
Your cousin, Omar

I reread the message several times, trying to decipher some hidden meaning from it. Of all the photographs he could have chosen, he picked one with me.

The front door opens, and I hear my father walk into Sousan and Ahmed's meeting.

What is this? he yells, and I can't tell by his tone if he's serious or joking.

I jump out of my chair and slide open the door to find Ahmed standing, his hands clenched and his jaw tight. Sousan stares, her eyes bouncing between the two men.

My father turns to look at me, and I am frightened by the severe look on his face.

Suddenly, he bursts into laughter.

Ahmed, Ahmed, my boy, I'm just joking. I know you know that I would kill you if you were to touch my Sousan before the wedding.

He wraps his arms around Ahmed and kisses him on the neck.

Sousan then laughs, covering her mouth with the fringed end of her hijab.

My mother touches my back and walks into the room.

Stop threatening the young man, or else he might be too frightened to ever give us grandchildren.

At this, Sousan's caramel skin turns white.

Yallah, my mother says to me. Get off that computer and help with the coffee.

The computer. Omar. Did she read what he wrote to me? Is that why her right eyebrow floats higher than the left?

My God, why didn't he write to me in English?

FOR THE NEXT few days, I avoid the computer and immerse myself in my books more than usual. I have been reading *Animal Farm*, a thin little book, for a week, but cannot focus on the words. Are these animals really talking? Whenever I am alone with my mother, I am convinced that she can hear my heartbeat, that she can feel my nervousness as it radiates out of my fingertips, out of the tops of my ears.

But she never mentions anything, and by the fifth night, after my parents and Sousan have gone to sleep, I decide to log on, to write the letter to Omar I have been reworking in my head, over and over, in Arabic.

Dearest Omar,

It is wonderful to hear from you. Please do not apologize about the photograph . . . I was so happy to see it as I too often think of those days. Just be sure my father doesn't hear of it! :)

Sousan is getting married to our cousin Ahmed. My father threatened to kill him should he touch her before the wedding . . . you should have seen the color of his cheeks!

Will you be coming back home for the wedding? I am sure that your mother and father miss you terribly. And I know that my family would love for you to celebrate with us.

I wanted to ask, do you remember how we used to write notes to each other in English? We had such little to say then—I wonder all that we could tell each other now.

God be with you,
Amal

My finger hovers over the mouse, and I reread the letter. While I can only hope that Omar is the same Omar who dreamed with me on my parents' carpet, how can I truly know?

Amal!

My mother's voice startles me, and I reflexively click, sending the message off.

Why are you awake? she asks as she walks toward me and the pale green glow of the computer.

Mama, I say, my voice shaking, I couldn't sleep.

She squints at the screen, trying to make out what it is I'm looking at.

You are going to go blind in this light, girl. Then who will want to marry you? She kisses my forehead and walks to the bathroom. Go to bed. You don't want your father catching you chatting with your cousin at this hour of the night.

And at this, I am speechless.

She closes the door, and I shut down the computer, rushing to get into bed before she reemerges.

THE NEXT MESSAGE I receive from Omar is, in fact, in English:

Dear Amal,

A wedding between Ahmed and Sousan? Mabrook! That is fantastic news. I will be at the party, inshallah. It would be so nice to see you. But poor Ahmed! I would not want to make your father angry.

I do remember writing letters to you. I found one in my photographs. You had written, "Jordan: the diamond in the desert." !!! Where did you possibly hear this? I will admit that after living in Amman I am beginning to question my love of this country. It seems to me that it is not a diamond at all, but completely desert. Even the sea here is dead!

I am sorry to be negative. I am so overwhelmed with exams that I don't have much time to enjoy this city. I hope to continue my studies in the UK, but it is only possible if I earn perfect marks.

Have you ever visited Amman? There is a park up on a hill that overlooks the entire city. It is so beautiful, especially at night. Next week, my friend Majdi is celebrating his birthday there, and we'll eat barbecued meats and play soccer, inshallah. I've been looking forward to it since my last exam.

Yours truly,
Omar

When I first read Omar's message, my heart drops. They are working him too hard, I think. They should not be putting him through all this pressure! If he is too stressed, he'll never get to England to complete his studies!

And then I think about what Omar has written: He wants to leave Jordan.

He wants to leave his family.

He wants to leave me.

I try to compose a response, but cannot.

How strange it is to be able to say so much when you have nothing to say, and then, when you finally have something to say, to be unable to say it.

Oh, Omar, it was so much easier when we were children.

Dear Omar,

Allah yabarak feek!

I am sorry to hear about the difficulties at the university. Al al-Bayt is very different . . . here, you receive high marks for being on time for an exam and, in some faculties, professors do not even show up to class!

I think you should come back to Mafrag. Being with your family will remind you of why Jordan really is a diamond in the desert, I promise.

What do you think the people are like in the UK? Do you think they are more like the characters in a Dickens novel? Or in an Austen? Have you read any of these novels? If you go there you must buy me as many books as you can.

Your friend's birthday celebration sounds so beautiful. I cannot remember the last time I ate barbecued meat.

Sincerely,
Amal

EVERY DAY WHEN I come home from the university, Sousan has a different shade of lipstick on her lips, or a new way to style her hair. She has been doing sit-ups for weeks, and bounces around our living room in front of a Lebanese exercise show.

My aunts are throwing her a party, one at which we will dye our hair with henna, eat platters of sweets, present her with gifts.

My father, he has been told, is forbidden from attending.

What are you going to do? he asks my mother. Kick me out of my own house?

Of course we will, she says in reply.

What am I supposed to eat? Where am I supposed to sleep? He brings up his hands in surrender. Surely God doesn't want me to be homeless!

This causes me to look up from my book.

What if I just sit and read here with Amal? Amal, do you have a copy in Arabic for me?

I nod. Yes, Baba, but you won't like it.

Why?

It's about pigs who take over a farm.

He raises his face to the ceiling, opens his palms to the sky. My God, what is happening in my home?

Oh, go to your brother's house, and leave us women be. You don't want to hear all the bedroom secrets we are going to tell Sousan!

My mother and I laugh, but both Sousan and my father are silent.

He stands, sighs, and heads out of the house, waving goodbye but not looking back. The door shuts behind him.

Mama! Sousan says.

My dear, it is nothing to be ashamed of. You will have duties as a wife! Yallah, come help me in the kitchen.

Alone once again, I return to my book, though my thoughts drift to Omar. Has he responded to my message? Do I have time to check?

Just as I move toward the computer, Aunt Hanan walks in, her hands full of packages and baklawa.

Oh, my sweet. Help me, please.

I set down my book and take the platters from her hands. She kisses me twice on both cheeks.

Is this in English? she asks, picking up the book. Clever, you.

I smile and lower my head.

Omar wants to complete his studies in England, she says.

Yes, I know, I say.

You do? She looks at me with the same raised eyebrow as my mother.

Oh, I—

I feel my face blush.

Sousan and my mother return from the kitchen, their hands full.

Amal! Go make the coffee.

The three of them embrace, offer praises of each other's desserts.

By the time I brew the coffee and return to the sitting room, the other aunts and cousins have arrived. We hug and kiss over and over, as if it is the last time we will meet.

Soon after, we sit in a crescent around Sousan. Each of us cradles, in our laps, a gift.

A pair of house slippers.

A set of towels embroidered with the words *Husband* and *Wife*.

A set of lacy red lingerie.

Sousan's whole body reddens.

Look, says Aunt Hanan, it's a perfect match!

Yes, but if he can't tell where her skin ends and the underwear begins, how will he take it off? my mother asks, her shoulders bent over a brazier of coals. She brings the hose of the argeela to her lips, drinks the syrupy smoke.

Aunt Hanan nudges Sousan in the ribs. Watch your mother, Sousan—she knows a thing or two about using her mouth.

We erupt with laughter.

My mother walks to the kitchen, shaking her head. I'm not denying a thing! she yells. I'm not denying a thing!

Later, we turn on MBC *The Voice* for music videos, tie scarves

around our hips, and dance. My mother and Aunt Hanan move
with such sexiness and ease, as does Nour. Sousan has her eyes
closed, dancing in her own world.

I wouldn't say that I am jealous of Sousan; no, not at all. But
when I think about her and Ahmed, I feel a particular loneliness
brewing inside my gut. Could marriage, the flood of love Sousan's
experiencing, drown this emptiness?

When Elissa's "Aa Baly Habibi" comes on, I shimmy my shoulders
and sing as loudly as I can: My love, I want to; My love, I want to.

My Amal, what is it that you want?

A WEEK GOES by without a response from Omar.

He is busy with his studies, I tell myself.

Sousan does sit-ups at my feet. The wedding is two days away.

You want him to do well, I think, so he can go to England.

England.

Amal, will you miss me?

Sousan leans on me, her hands on my knees.

I swallow the lump building in my throat, feel the tears pooling
in my eyes.

She dives onto the couch with me, nuzzles her head on my shoulder, laces her fingers into mine.

My mother walks in with glasses of yogurt to find the two of us
sniffling.

Oh, my loves.

She wraps her arms around our shoulders, rocks us back and
forth with our temples close to one another's as she did when we
were small.

My father joins next, kissing each of us on the tops of our heads.

It is hard to be surrounded by so much love and yet feel so out of place.

BY THE EVE of the wedding, I have yet to hear from Omar.

Surely if he were back in Mafrag, he would have messaged me. Surely Aunt Hanan would have brought him over this afternoon for coffee. Surely I would know he was near. So where is he?

And then I realize: No, of course we didn't hear from him. It is the day before a wedding! There have been so many details to align and organize before the big day that none of us have had a moment to relax. Omar was being polite, I tell myself, by not announcing his arrival. He wants us to focus our attention on the bride, on the last night we'll have her in our home. And so I happily join my mother in an orbit around Sousan, painting her nails and combing her hair.

But that evening, after my mother and father and Sousan have turned off the lights and fallen into their beds, I log on to Facebook. Tomorrow, Omar will be there, celebrating with the men. While it is true we will likely not see each other, we will be dancing, singing, celebrating at the exact same moment in adjacent rooms, all in honor of Sousan and Ahmed's marriage.

Marriage.

I cannot keep my face from smiling.

I have over fifty notifications, and thirteen messages. I pace myself, going through the notifications first. No need to rush, I say. If he's written you, it will be there. Just be yourself.

A friend from university has tagged me and thirty others in a pic of Queen Rania. The words *Charm. Beauty. Confidence. Queen.* float beside her smiling face. Nearly everyone has commented, offering praises to our royal family. Nour has invited me to play

Bubble Witch Saga and *CastleVille* and *Mall World*, games I have always wanted to play but which never seem to load on my screen.

I take a deep breath, click on my messages. Several from Nour, Sousan, Aliya. Nothing from Omar.

I go to his profile page, scan through his feed. His last status update was over two weeks ago. No new pictures have been added. And while friends have seemed to write on his wall, he hasn't as much as liked any of the posts. Where is he?

I write him a message, hoping that he is online and will reply.

Dear Omar,

Are you in Mafrag? The wedding is tomorrow!!

Before you go back to Amman, you must come over for coffee. My parents will insist.

Love,
Amal

After I click send, I think about the word *love* and begin to regret having used it. Am I being too direct? Will he think that, because I mentioned my parents, I want him to formally discuss our relationship with them? (Do we even have a "relationship"?) I sit in the darkness for an hour, reading our correspondence over and over to look for clues, hints that he isn't really interested in me—that he was just being nice. It can't be the case, I tell myself. Why would he have said that it would be so nice to see me? And why would he write to me in English? I wait for him, but there is no response. I crawl into bed, unable to sleep. My feet shake under the sheets.

Then I begin to get angry. Why is he ignoring me? Is he trying to torture me? And almost instantly, with these self-centered thoughts, the worst images come to mind: ambulances, a jail cell, the dead man in the road in downtown Amman. If only Omar had stayed here in Mafrag, I think, he would be protected by the clan.

Amal? Are you awake? Sousan asks.

I stop my turning, try to lay quiet, still.

Amal?

Yes, Sou Sou, I'm awake.

I can't sleep, she says. I'm too happy to sleep.

After some years, after both Sousan and I have children, children who play at our feet while we sip cigarettes and tea, I'll think back to this moment, to this last instance when we lay parallel to each other in our beds.

THINGS ARE MUCH quieter around our house now that the wedding festivities are over. In some ways, it is a relief; we don't have any more crafts to complete, any more paper boxes to score and fold, any more makeup or hairstyles to experiment with. But in other ways, there is an aimlessness to our daily activities. It is strange how one can plan an event for months, look forward to something for years, it seems, just to have it end.

My mother tries to occupy her time with little projects, with repairs and hobbies she has been putting off for ages. She has even bought a *Learn English Today!* workbook, but whenever she tries to read the short paragraphs or copy down the new vocabulary words, she falls asleep with her cheek on her fist, her mouth open. My father, when returning home from work, slumps on a cushion in front of the TV, perpetually flipping through the channels. News reports about protests in Amman flash on the screen, and while these cause my ears to perk up, he seems as uninterested in them as he is in soap operas and American films.

I spend the bulk of my days at the university. It's not that there is much for me to do there either, but now, with Sousan and Ahmed in their own apartment, our home feels too spacious, too dark. It is as if the building itself is grieving the loss of a loved one.

Except when it is time for afternoon tea. Now, my mother and I have two guests to entertain: Aunt Hanan and Sousan. And for those few hours, it feels lighter, brighter inside.

Oh, Sou Sou, our bride! my mother says, squeezing Sousan from the side.

Really, habibiti, the wedding was perfect, says Aunt Hanan. And your jewelry is so lovely!

Sousan brings her hand to her chest, fingering one of the delicate gold necklaces Ahmed presented to her at the reception. Each piece is adorned with tiny pink stones clustered to form the shape of a heart.

It was really all I've ever wanted, she says.

And this is how it goes. We light cigarettes, and brew sweetened tea, and reminisce over our favorite moments of the party. How Sousan and Ahmed sat on a gilded couch at the front of the room, the two of them radiating happiness. How the women joined hands to form a circle, smiling and dancing and celebrating our beloveds. How, before departing to the men's party, Ahmed bowed to the crowd and whispered into Sousan's ear. And how she smiled and floated in a cloud of white toward the center, where we surrounded her and danced, my mother and Aunt Hanan yelling to the beat: Yes! Yes! Sou Sou, yes!

I have a memory of the wedding that I do not share with the others. After Sousan joined the women in the circle, she closed her eyes, raised her hands, and shook her hips. At that moment, I thought to myself, Maybe Omar was just kidding around. Maybe he wanted to make his appearance a surprise. And maybe, I thought, when Ahmed reenters the men's party, Omar will be the one to clap him on the shoulder, to try to sneak a glance into our room. I moved beside my sister and followed her lead; the two of us held hands and danced, each smiling because of a young man in the adjoining reception.

How foolish of me. Omar wasn't there, I learned the next day, and he still hasn't written me back.

That night, once Aunt Hanan and Sousan have left, and my mother and father go to sleep, I decide to act. I cannot just wait here, hoping he will show up one day. And so, for the first time, I tell Omar a lie.

Dear Omar,

Keefik, habibi? We were sorry to hear that you didn't make it to Sousan and Ahmed's wedding. It was really so beautiful. But we know how busy you are with your studies. I hope that you are giving yourself at least a little time to relax!

I am writing to tell you that I will be in Amman next Sunday. There is a book I need to buy, one that the stores in Mafrag do not have. Would you be able to meet me for coffee? I do not know the city at all, but if you know of a place near the city center, I will try to find it.

With love,
Amal

✦

I AM RESTLESS after sending this, and become careless around the house. I begin to bicker with my mother over the tiniest things, blaming her for my own clumsiness. By the next evening, she suggests that I spend a few nights with Sousan, even though it would mean imposing myself on the newlyweds. I first scoff at the idea, but begin to consider it as I log on to Facebook late that night.

I have one message; it's from Omar.

> My dear Amal,
>
> It would be an honor to have coffee with you. I cannot believe that you will be here . . . or that your parents will let you travel alone! They must know how clever you are. Let's meet at Jara Café on Rainbow Street, around 1 p.m. It will be wonderful to see you.
>
> Love,
> Omar

I hear my father stirring in his bedroom, and then a particularly violent sneeze. I panic and quickly shut down the computer without logging off or closing any programs and rush to get into my bed. I lay in the darkness for a long while.

THE FOLLOWING SUNDAY, I wake and get myself ready as if I am going to the university. But I have a difficult time deciding what to wear. I put on multiple outfits, look in the mirror disapprovingly, then peel them off and toss them on Sousan's empty bed. (I don't want it to be too obvious that I am trying hard, but I am really trying hard!) In the end, I decide to go simple, conservative, with a splash of color: a taupe jilbab, one with shiny brass buttons and a belt that cinches at the waist, a watercolor hijab, and pale pink flats with roses on the toe. I fasten my scarf with pins adorned with tiny fabric roses, and wear the slightest smudge of mascara.

I move through the house quickly, downing my coffee at the sink, and search for something clean and easy—a pastry, a piece of fruit—to grab for the bus.

My mother watches me from the entrance to the kitchen, but I do not notice her presence until she speaks.

What's the rush?

I drop a spoon. Mamma, I—

You look nice.

I avoid eye contact by rummaging through the fridge, where I find an orange. I have a tutoring session with a first-year, I say. Her English is horrible.

She kisses me on the cheek as I walk past. Be careful, she says. And, here, take some money for lunch. You have to eat more than that!

I HAD FORGOTTEN about the hills in Amman. I knew about them—of course I did—but it was as if my mind didn't remember that it remembered until I saw them once again. As I walk from the bus station to downtown, I notice how the square white buildings planted onto the steep hillsides appear to be stacked atop one another, how the cedar trees reach like arms toward the sky.

The air is cool and crisp and brighter here than in Mafrag, I think, and I am happy.

In the distance, I can see the Citadel atop the hill to my right, and the Roman Theatre to my left. It's curious to me how these landmarks look essentially the same as the picture in my mind, but ever so slightly shrunken. While it is true that I have grown, I wonder if, somehow, these images have bloomed in my mind, if they also have grown in the past thirteen years since their roots took hold in my memory.

I pass a string of souvenir shops. Scarves hang from the awnings and, on the sidewalk, postcards sit in spinners. It is then I get the idea to look for the one that says *Jordan: The Diamond in the Desert*, and give it to Omar during our meeting. He'd think it so funny! I turn the metal rack, looking for the phrase. I see camels and bedouins—it is strange to me that tourists buy these pictures of people who look so much like my family members. There are pictures of Petra and the Dead Sea, places I've never been, of the beach at Aqaba and the king and queen. One postcard says, *Jordanian and proud of it*. Another has a picture of a camel in a niqab and says, *Jordanian Princess*. (I cannot tell if I am to laugh or to be offended.) I see the shopkeeper sweeping in the back, and I ask him for help.

He leads me to the selection of English-language postcards. He picks one and hands it to me, but, to my disappointment, it is not the one I want. Instead, it reads, *I'm famous in Amman*. I tell him the phrase again, and he says, This is what I have. What else do you want?

I apologize and leave quickly, a little flustered. Of course, it is silly of me to think that one postcard I saw thirteen years ago would still be there. I cannot even be certain that it is the same shop. As I walk toward the city center, I feel as if all the shopkeepers—the juice sellers and spice merchants—are watching me. I am grateful when I reach a busier portion of the block, where men and women peruse the stores and vegetables for sale on the side of the road. I check my mobile: I have just over an hour until I am to meet Omar.

Prayer has ended, and people flow out of the mosque and onto the square. I ask a woman in a black abaya if she can direct me to Rainbow Street. She hesitates, and then asks a friend, who speaks so loudly that a pious-looking man nearby can hear, and they all debate for a few minutes which is the best way for me to go.

Could I walk there? I ask.

You could, the man says, but it's a ways up. He points to a nearby hill, one that looks as steep as a mountain from where we stand. Take care, sister, he says.

I begin my ascent. While I am not used to much exercise, it is difficult to tell whether the pounding in my chest is from a lack of stamina or from the excitement of seeing Omar for the first time in I-cannot-remember-how-long. By the time I reach the first landing, though, I most certainly am out of breath. I pause to get some rest, and turn to see the progress I've made, which is much more than I had expected. I can see all of downtown below me: the mosque and the Roman Theatre and the road that leads to the bus station. The Citadel is perched on a hill opposite me, and while I am not quite at its level, I feel elevated, amazed. To think that I took the two-hour bus ride here, by myself, without help or instructions from anyone! My parents would be furious if they knew. But, maybe, after they got over their initial shock and worry, they'd feel pride, confidence in what I am capable of. It is so wonderful to be here, to see these places that I remember from when I was quite young, to be in the same city that Omar lives in. I wonder if he lives nearby, if he buys his vegetables and meat from the market near the mosque, if he has greeted those same people who gave me directions.

At the same time, the thought of my childhood trip and Omar

causes a loneliness to creep inside my chest. What if it's not the same between us?

Dear Amal, why are you afraid?

AN IVY-COVERED PATH leads me to the next staircase, flanked on both sides by a rose garden. An orange cat lies in the sun, sleeping.

Finally, I find myself on Rainbow Street. It is a beautiful street, much cleaner and neater than the city center or Mafrag, and the storefronts all have signage in English: CANTALOUPE, WAZZUP DOG, WAFFLE HOUSE, Q. The street is less crowded than downtown, and every person is so lovely and chic, I assume they must all be foreign. Two women with flowing blond hair and high heels walk toward me with ice cream cones. They are so beautiful and stylish I can hardly stand to be near them. I have never met a foreigner, though I read about them all the time. Here is your chance, I say to myself. Tell them, Hello. But as they approach, I realize that they aren't speaking English or French, but Arabic. I smile and nod as they pass, but I cannot tell if they can even see me from behind their large sunglasses. I am suddenly very aware of how small I am, how my jilbab—even though belted—hangs shapeless off my frame. I must seem so quaint to them.

The café Omar has suggested is more wonderful than I could have imagined: an open rooftop overlooking downtown, with fountains and tiny tables surrounded by colorful embroidered pillows. A man stands at the front gate, nodding at customers as they walk in. He stares at me for several seconds before asking, Yes?

Excuse me. I am meeting a friend here.

He raises his eyebrows and calls over a waiter. I cannot hear what they are saying. What I can hear, however, is my rural accent, something I never even considered before.

I interrupt: Sorry—can't I go inside? I am early, but my friend will be here soon.

The waiter leads me to a table, sets down two menus.

He says, I'm sorry, miss, but we only have menus in English.

And this is what I do not have the courage to say in response: That's no problem, sir. I speak English quite well, actually.

But instead I lower my head, mutter, Okay, under my breath, and study the menu until he leaves.

OMAR IS LATE. I read and reread the menu over and over. How I would love to smoke argeela here while I wait, but I know I cannot. For one thing, I do not want to speak to that waiter again and, for another, I could never smoke in a place so open, so public.

When he finally arrives, I am no longer upset or embarrassed. He walks in smiling, with his hands in the pockets of his light gray jeans. His eyes are just the color I remember them to be.

I cannot hide my grin.

We greet each other formally, as if we were strangers and not family. We do not hug or shake hands or touch at all. When we sit, the waiter returns. Omar orders us two glasses of honeydew juice. I try to take slow, steady breaths.

Sorry to keep you waiting, he says, looking directly at me.

I lower my gaze and say, Don't worry.

But then I decide that it is silly of me to come all the way here to not look at him in the face. This is Omar! The one I think fondly of every day.

I bring my eyes level with his. It's so nice to see you. When was the last time?

He leans back in his chair and thinks for a moment. I don't know!

As we sit in awe, marveling over the fact that we are both in Amman together (this is what I'm thinking, at least), silence creeps between us. We begin to look around, chasing each other's gaze.

After some time, I sigh and say, Wow, this place is really beautiful.

You like it? he asks.

Yes, very much so. Do you come here often?

No, he says. I've never been here before. I don't usually leave the area near the university. I asked a friend to suggest a place where we should meet.

I wonder, Did Omar tell his friend about me?

It is so beautiful here, I say again. We have nothing like this in Mafrag.

To which he laughs. There are many things here that you do not have in Mafrag.

The waiter brings our drinks in etched goblets with long straws.

So lovely! I say, and take a sip. It is syrupy and thick and gets caught in my throat as I try to swallow. I cough for what seems like several moments, and Omar looks at me with concern. His stare makes it even more difficult for me to catch my breath.

Finally, I calm down, and he lightly touches my arm. Are you okay?

I nod my head yes, and try to prevent the tears that have pooled in my eyes from running down my cheeks.

There must be bones in there, he says.

I look at him with confusion. Bones?

He smiles. It's something my father used to say when we were little. You've never heard it before?

No, I say.

Omar pulls a package of cigarettes from his pocket and begins to smoke. I watch his hands, notice the way he holds the cigarette between his third and fourth fingers as opposed to the second and third. When he cups his hand around the flame of the lighter, I see that his fingernails have been chewed to the quick. He is the gentle and bright boy I remember from my childhood, I think, but something is different about him. When he smiles, his eyes no longer pinch at the sides. Strands of gray streak his otherwise black hair. It is then I realize that we've forgotten how to be ourselves around each other. It has been too many years, I think, for us to even speak.

But why was it so much easier on Facebook? That felt natural and real.

Can we speak in English? I ask, hoping to lighten the mood, to bring us back to a time when we were close.

He hesitates in Arabic. Amal, I—

Oh, please! Like we did when we were young.

We never spoke, he said. Just passed notes.

Well, let's speak. I have no one to practice with at home. You must get to speak English all the time here.

Not really, he says, and lights another cigarette. Really, I can't. I am too embarrassed of my accent.

But, if you want to be a doctor in England, you'll—

I know, I know, he interrupts me. Please, it is difficult for me now. English makes my brain even more tired than it already is.

I nod and drink more honeydew—this time, slowly. I then concentrate on my own hands in my lap. On the tiny lines crisscrossing the tops of my knuckles.

I'm sorry, he says. Please don't be upset.

I try not to be, but my vision blurs, and tiny droplets of tears fall onto my lap, darkening the fabric of my jilbab in a kind of constellation. I didn't expect it to be like this.

And it is then I hear Omar say to me, in English: How are you, Miss Amal?

I wipe the tears from my face and smile. His accent is atrocious. I am very well, Mister Omar. And yourself?

I am tired.

I tilt my head to the side. Tired? Are you not happy to see me?

Oh, I am happy to see you. But I am also very tired.

You study too much.

Not enough.

How not enough? You are always studying!

Trust me, he says. Then, Did you find your book?

My book? I ask, nearly forgetting the lie I had written him. Alas, no. The bookseller didn't have it.

And you came all this way? What a shame!

I shrug. Does he really think it's a shame?

I am sad when it is time for Omar to return to the university, and me to the bus station. Not because I am going back to Mafrag and will not see him for some time, though that is certainly part of it, but because I am realizing that shared memories aren't quite enough. I never would have imagined, after all these years, that this person whom I've felt so connected to (without as much as exchanging a word!) could be so distant, so lost. I am sorry that I pushed him to speak English, that I held on to this tiny nugget from our childhood for so long. I am sorry that I wasn't prepared for him to have grown or changed in a way that diverged from my imaginings of him, and that I didn't know how to respond to it.

I don't tell him any of this, of course. And so we shake hands and walk our separate ways.

Why do you think we've been put on this Earth?
What is it you want most out of life?
Amal, what makes you cry?

BACK AT OUR house, my father lies in bed while my mother makes tea. I curl my legs under myself on the couch and light a cigarette.

Amal, habibiti, are you all right?

My mother sets a glass in my hands and sits down beside me. My dear, please say something.

I look at her, but I don't know anything I could possibly say.

She leans her head into mine, grabs the back of my neck. We sit like this for some minutes, and I feel her tears mixing with mine.

I'm here, Amal. I'm here when you need me.

AFTER MY MOTHER and father go to bed, I log on to Facebook.

I have sixteen messages: three from Nour, six from Sousan, seven from Aliya. These I leave in my inbox, unopened, as I search for Omar's page. After a minute or so, it loads, looks the same as it usually does. There aren't any new comments, any new posts on his wall, any evidence of activity at all. I can't say that I expected there to be, but it saddens me all the same.

There was a time when I didn't know if Omar remembered me,

when I didn't know if he and I would ever write letters to each other again. I try to go back, to imagine that he and I hadn't yet become Facebook friends, that I hadn't found that picture of us when we were children.

Sousan and Ahmed are smiling, sitting nervously in the guest room.

My mother is bumbling around the kitchen, clanking spoons against aluminum pots, preparing coffee for us all.

I click through Omar's pics for the first time.

Omar in front of the gates of the university, wearing sunglasses and making a backwards peace sign.

A Barcelona football jersey.

Omar in a red keffiyeh.

It was such a beautiful feeling, to have that kind of hope in another person.

Emily Chammah is an assistant editor at American Short Fiction, where she co-organizes the Insider Prize, a contest for incarcerated writers in Texas. She is the creator of the online travel guide Weird and Wonderful Cairo and works as an immigration paralegal in Bay Ridge, Brooklyn.

EDITOR'S NOTE

Katherine Magyarody's "Goldhawk," which was the winner of the fiction category in *The Malahat Review*'s 2016 Open Season Awards, is a subtle story about twenty-first-century office environments. Dinara, an immigrant, from a former totalitarian state, is the only woman on her team at an IT company. (I imagine it to be located in the 905 calling area, the band of edge cities girdling Toronto.) Her much younger male peers, most of whom have "student loans to repay, mortgages, children to raise," resent that she's survived repeated downsizings, attributing this not to the quality of her work but to her gender.

The sighting of a gold-colored hawk in the trees unifies the team—Dinara included—as they watch it in awe from a wall of sun-drenched windows. This "fellow" feeling, however, is short-lived.

I love this story because it captures the light-flooded sterility of today's workplace, which conditions employees to pay lip service to equity while sequestering themselves in sublimated misogyny and xenophobia. This is not the Canada that our apparent openness to others promulgates, and Magyarody is to be congratulated for showing how such forces continue to undermine the social praxis of everyday life. The symbolism of the hawk sits lightly on her story, as lightly and as elusively as Dinara herself, who evinces a protective self-determination in not allowing herself to be too well understood. "Goldhawk" causes us to reflect on the intractable, fallible nature of our assumptions and freedoms.

John Barton, editor
The Malahat Review

GOLDHAWK

Katherine Magyarody

DINARA AKHMATOVA SURVIVED the purges. First the company laid off the lazy and the incompetent. Dinara, with a row of programming manuals and her cut-glass award for ten years of service the only ornaments in her cubicle, was not even looked at by management. Or rather, their eyes passed over her while the fingertips of one hand flew across the keyboard and the other cradled the newest prototype. When the company still hemorrhaged money, they began cutting entire projects. The aspirational ventures, the innovations that had made their name. Dinara, slight of body and flexible of mind, refocused all her attention onto product development. Once the mandarin class of employees had been cut loose, the company went through each remaining team and discarded one in three. She came in early and stayed later than anyone. She survived.

Her colleagues did not like her for it.

"It's because she's a woman," Sergei muttered. "It looks good for the diversity profile."

"She's gotta be . . . old," Leroy said. He worked a few cubicles down from her. He was not sure how old Dinara was, but surely the young needed jobs more than someone his mother's age. He and his team had student loans to repay, mortgages, children to raise.

Dinara had . . . well, beyond the silver Toyota Camry she drove to work, he was not sure what she had.

"It's because she's a . . ." a student intern began. He was just beginning to learn the habits of the company and wanted badly to contribute his first gossip "around the water cooler," a phenomenon described in the books on business culture he had pored over. Instead of finishing, he rolled his eyes. He could not find the words. But the others nodded, because what Dinara was precisely was hard to tell.

She was, indeed, a woman. That was easy. In a company of computer programmers and product testers who wore scrubby polo shirts and khakis to work, Dinara wore long gauzy skirts and soft, pastel cardigans that emphasized her birdlike figure. She wore dangling silver earrings below her short dark hair. She was soft-spoken and her voice was high. The single time she had been known to make a joke was at a meeting where a new employee named Nureyev was introduced. "Will you develop superior techniques so beautifully and then defect?" she asked; her impish smile narrowly survived the awkward silence. She then added, "You share your name with a *kak eta* . . . wondrous man of dance." The men had laughed for her benefit; even though they resented her, they could not bear to see her softness damaged in public.

How old was she? It was difficult to guess. Her hair was as black as her eyes. If someone looked closely—which no one bothered to do—they might have seen fine lines around her eyes, across her forehead, connecting the corners of her nostrils to the tips of her smiling lips. Where she was from was equally difficult to tell. She spoke quietly, quickly, and not long enough for the others to catch her accent. Her name looked a little Russian, with its *-ova* another testament to her femininity, but she looked not at all Russian, with

her olive skin and low broad cheekbones. Nor did she possess any
motherly rapport with the gang of young Russian product testers.
Indeed, she seemed to avoid them, to cling to the shadows and corners when they walked by bragging loudly and unselfconsciously
about their computers, their cars.

Had anyone asked Dinara what she was, she would have said,
"Oh, darling, I am so *tired*."

Or perhaps she would remain silent, because admitting to fa-
tigue might insinuate her inability to make the quota. She had
chosen this country; this was the end point of her third and final
migration. She was determined to prove that the evaporation of her
savings in immigration fees and the melting away of her untranslat-
able credentials, as she passed through the atmosphere of another
language and culture, had been worthwhile.

She had, once upon a time, studied the stars at a national institute. She loved the sky. But penetrating the unknown of the
universe was small compensation. Each of her choices was moni-
tored, analyzed, cataloged, and stripped of mystery. Now, having
escaped, she took pleasure in knowing that her work contributed
to protecting privacy, a privilege she had grown up without. Now
she protected the privacy of unknown others even as she protected
her own.

There were other benefits to her work. The building was beige
and putty colored inside, but every morning when Dinara drove to
the office she watched the sun stain the broad sky as it rose. As the
light built in intensity from purplish blue to green, pink, orange,
gold, she would see the silhouettes of the trees emerge from the
uniform darkness. Where she had grown up, there was only village
and wilderness, city and wilderness, crop field and wilderness. The
wilderness was where the land was too tough for cultivation, where

people threw their empty bottles and cigarette butts. The government had sternly encouraged reproduction, so there was only occasionally a distended condom, translucent and miraculous.

In this country, she had a sense that even the pines and the sumac and the tall grass along the corridor of the highway were imbued with love. It was with wonder that one morning in early spring she spotted a group of orange-outfitted men picking up trash from the median. She thought of calling her mother and telling her, but her mother, a kerchiefed lady rooted to her particular patch of land and no other, would have simply shaken her head at the insanity of the West.

And truly, Dinara thought as she waited for her code to run, in comparison to her mother's years loading and unloading bread from trucks, selling bread and eating it, there was something insane about a room of people who spent their days staring at small boxes. About people who spent their days in silence punctuated by the tap of plastic keys.

"Hawk!" someone cried.

"Whoa! Hawk!" Another took up the cry. Around her, the men were leaping from their chairs and running.

Dinara paused at her typing, her heart beating hard. Was this some sort of North American engineering term? She looked up at her row of programming-language manuals. No, she wouldn't find the answer in her reference guides. She stood up and began walking toward the windows, where a crowd was forming. *Hawk*, she was sure, was some slang a boy genius had invented to keep some people from understanding. She hugged her elbows and moved slowly, to give herself time to think, to plan.

But her pace quickened as she saw that the others were not in a circle, facing inward, but in a cluster facing the cruelly bright sky.

"Hawk," Samy said quietly, he whom Dinara often overheard unabashedly discussing the pliancy of women's bodies over the phone in pungent Hebrew. Perhaps he thought no one understood him. Perhaps he didn't care. Now, Samy's face was almost reverent. He pointed.

Dinara quickly put on her glasses, her secret vanity conceding to her desire for knowledge.

And she saw.

There, on the Norway pine, ten feet from the wall of the building, perched a great golden bird.

"Hawk," Dinara breathed.

Someone—Mo, the babyish university intern—tapped the glass. The bird's head turned instantly, locating the source of the sound. And then it swooped down at the winter-pale faces. A hushed gasp rose and a few at the front of the crowd stumbled backward, dreading the sharp smack of flesh against glass, of bones breaking. Dinara stepped forward to see better.

In the last moment, the bird swerved away to the right. It soared high, wheeled in a circle, and dove again. This time, it pulled itself directly upward. Gold plumes flashed as it rose, wings churning as it turned.

"That thing is going to smash itself into the window," Samy said, stepping away.

"She will not," Dinara said. "She is . . . too smart."

Sergei shrugged, turned. "You see it, sometimes, in the parking lot. The birds break their necks against the glass. It'll happen either now or later."

The others watched in silence as the raptor ducked to the left and continued to circle, flexing its talons. Rise and fall, rise and fall, rise and fall.

Reginald Tau reminded them of the client meeting. "Sixteen hours, people," he said.

They peeled away from the window, returned to the fluorescent depths of the building. Dinara was the last to retreat. For the rest of the afternoon, she could see people surreptitiously tipping their chairs back to check whether the bird was still there.

But the hawk seemed to have lost interest and vanished.

The hands on the wall clock ticked past five o'clock, then six o'clock in the evening. The creature had not reappeared.

"Is it a goldhawk?" she asked Leroy as the rest started to trickle homeward. She noticed he had a Wikipedia page on raptors nestled discreetly beside his work email. Dinara didn't know many animal names, but Goldhawk was the name of a street in her neighborhood.

"No such thing," he said, pulling up the page. He looked smug, because he had figured something out before her. "What we saw was a red-tailed hawk. They're actually not supposed to be this far south and west."

"That is not what we saw," she said softly. "Our hawk was gold."

Leroy moved his jaw slightly left, slightly right, not enjoying her resistance.

"Sorry, Dinara. There's no such thing."

She put on her glasses again and leaned close into the screen to look. Then she straightened.

"Hmm," she said, a noncommittal noise to satisfy his pride. She began packing up her laptop.

EACH MORNING, DINARA parked her car (a car—what a luxury it had once seemed, now what a necessity it had become) and stared up at the pine trees that ringed the asphalt lot, watched as they stood rigid in the still air or swayed with the wind.

Each evening, her walk from the doors of the building to her distant corner of the parking lot was consolation for the hours in stale air reeking with male sweat and anxiety. That night, like every night, in the space between the hiss of the automated exit and the gentle slam of her car door, she prayed for one more day, one more week, one more year, until her children finished university and could support themselves, until she did not carry the burden of their three souls upon her back.

In the twilight, she saw the glint of feathers, heard the rustle of a disturbed branch. She looked up and saw a round unblinking eye watching her. She stood still, feeling her fingertips grow cold in the night air. It was gold, she thought triumphantly, not at all like the picture Leroy had shown her. Not that she would tell him—she would let him be satisfied in his ignorance.

The hawk tilted its head once, as if to concede to Dinara a lack of danger. Its head ducked down and she heard the rip of tendon and muscle. It must have found a squirrel. As the hawk pulled at its meal, the branch trembled. Dinara thought she could just see the clustered branches of a nest.

She would not tell the men she had seen the hawk's secret place.

Katherine Magyarody is a postdoctoral fellow at Texas A&M University. She completed her PhD in English at the University of Toronto in 2016. In her fiction she explores the personal, familial, and cultural histories that we remember, and the secrets that keep us awake at night. She is working on a collection of short stories and two novel manuscripts.

EDITORS' NOTE

"Galina" is a beautiful story told by a skilled and talented writer. We were captivated by Angela Ajayi's descriptions of a fictional exclusion zone near the site of a nuclear accident in Ukraine, and carried away by the sureness of her voice and the richness of her characters. What made the story stand out from the many others we read was Ajayi's penetrating depiction of a mother-daughter relationship marked by history and time. In the author's hands, a simple reunion in a kitchen and a view outside to a cherry tree become menacing and urgent. Galina has fled Nigeria and her marriage only to find her motherland poisoned and changed forever.

We read about 1,500 unsolicited short stories each year, always with an eye for work by new writers. It is not often that we find writing of the quality in this story. We are not surprised that she was chosen for an award, and we are very happy with the confirmation of our faith in this story and in Angela's talent and hard work.

Vern Miller, publisher
Rachel Swearingen, guest fiction editor
Fifth Wednesday Journal

GALINA

Angela Ajayi

"You were like a bird," Galina's mother said to her. "The kind that came during the summer when the trees were filled with fruit. Then you flew south, after a coolness had settled in the morning air, to a land so distant that I couldn't even imagine it."

Galina laughed at the comparison, apt as it was and described so poetically, as they drank tea in her mother's kitchen. She looked out the window by the old wooden fence and her eyes fell on a cherry tree dotted with forbidden fruit.

It had been a month since Galina had returned from Nigeria for good. On her first visit, guards holding rifles at the checkpoint two miles away had warned her that her mother's village, Zhovtnevoe, was in an exclusion zone, that the radiation levels were still high even eight years after the blast at nearby Tarkov Nuclear Power Plant.

"Try to get your mother out. Don't drink the water or eat the vegetables and fruit," they had said as they stamped the date on her pass.

But Galina hadn't dwelled on their words. She wanted to live for the moment, shabby as it was. She laughed again, and her voice sounded cheery and high-pitched like a child's.

"Let me see," she asked her mother in the kitchen. "And how else am I like a bird?"

"I know—your face!" The words escaped through chapped lips, leaping out of a mouth framed by wrinkles with specks of dirt in them.

Galina knew her mother hadn't meant it as a cruel gibe. Over the years, she had begun to look birdlike. Her eyes, always large, appeared larger now, and her nose was longer, pointier at its tip. Lately her lips had thinned and were barely visible.

"Pity," her mother said again. "You were such a beauty. I couldn't keep the boys away. I wanted to lock you in the house and keep you there forever. Then you left."

"But, Ma—" Galina protested. Her tea had gotten cold, and she pushed the cup away. It left a brown stain on the white tablecloth.

"You went away, and each time you came back during the summer you looked a little different."

"I got older," Galina said, but she knew this was not the whole truth and that her decade in Nigeria had changed her irreversibly. These days she laughed easily at the most inopportune times; she cried just as easily. And when she tried lovemaking again, after meeting Olexa at Perchok School in nearby Drabov where she now lived and taught geometry, she grew so anxious that she stopped returning his calls.

"You're broken, Galochka. I don't know what ended your marriage, but you've lost your way," her mother said, as she poured herself more tea and sipped it without adding more milk or sugar.

Galina wondered when her mother had become this forthright, this blunt with her delivery. She averted her eyes from the stain and looked out the window again toward the cherry tree a few feet away. She could swear the leaves looked bigger than when she was a young girl, their fresh dark green color glistening under the sunlight. A barn swallow swooped down on one of the branches and rested there, bejeweled by its bluish-red feathers.

"I'm not broken," Galina said. But her voice wavered, revealing the true weight of her insecurities. She had come undone in a way that couldn't be measured. She might have begun to lose her mind in Nigeria after learning of her husband Umaru's secret— plunged into a darkness that only her motherland could retrieve her from. And that was why she'd bought herself a one-way ticket with the money she had saved from decorating wedding cakes. She had told Umaru that their marriage was over and flew away that day.

The swallow on the tree lowered its short neck and pecked at a cherry, digging into the red flesh and exposing the brown pit. Melancholy hung in the air. Galina cleared her throat. The sound she emitted was not the usual hoarse-sounding one—it was as if she had just whistled a happy tune. Her mother, whose hearing never failed, turned her head and leaned closer. A whiff of raw garlic hit Galina's nose.

"It's not my life I'm worried about now," Galina said. "We need to get you out of here. The longer you stay, the more likely you'll die from cancer. Just look at the leaves on that cherry tree. Look how big they are. Next year, they will double in size."

"Nonsense," her mother said. "Even with the radiation, things won't change that quickly. Besides, I'm almost seventy-five—I'll die of old age soon."

Galina shook her head. The years had not been kind to either one of them. Her mother had grown more isolated, more certain of her impending demise. Her only other visitor was a brother, Ivan, who lived in another village outside the exclusion zone. These days, guilt, dull but insistent, had crept into Galina's heart, and she wondered if both their lives would have worked out better if she'd stayed closer to her mother.

"I dug up some more potatoes this morning. I'll make us some borscht for lunch," her mother said.

"We really shouldn't eat the vegetables," Galina said, but her mother shushed her.

"A woman has to eat. I won't starve to death like my grandparents almost did. I've eaten hundreds of those potatoes and I'm still here." She stood up and reached for her walking stick. Her hands had become unusually large, and her fingers looked bulbous at the tips, but she gripped the walking stick with such ease. The old woman was stubborn, even in the face of a life lived semilegally in isolation.

"I'm going to the cellar to get the potatoes and beets," her mother said.

"Let me help you," Galina said.

But her mother raised a hand in the air and shook it as she walked away. This movement startled the swallow outside the window on the cherry tree, and it darted up toward the blue sky, leaving the fruit half eaten.

THE FIRST DAY Galina had visited her mother, she had killed a swallow with her car. It had happened a mile from the checkpoint. She had driven through Shramkovka, past the general store where she used to buy fresh bread and chunks of sweet halvah. The store stood empty, its windows clouded over with dust. She had come upon Baba Dasha's house, a stone's throw from the store, abandoned. Then Galina had driven out of the small town and onto the tarred highway. Alongside her, the fields that were once filled with wheat, usually bent by the wind, were overgrown with weeds. As she neared her mother's village, she had been relieved to see that the forest of fir trees that lined part of the road looked unchanged. She maneuvered the car onto the muddy road that led to her mother's house, and it struck her that the road appeared less ugly with fewer tire marks.

The Shurkas' house was barely hanging on—its windows dust-filled, its thatched roof caving in, the windows still lined with a few possessions that were left behind in the hasty evacuation. Outside the house, a sandpit, in which Galina had played as a child, was strewn with plastic toys. She remembered her childhood, when the summer days had been bright and long and filled with playing or fishing by the pond behind their house. She would climb trees or run through cornfields, emerging flushed and winded. It had been a joyful time until the summer she was thirteen, when her father died of a heart attack on a train.

Her mother had howled into the night, beating the floor with her fists. "My Vityok, not my Vityok!"

And yet with each new day, Galina and her mother had fed the chickens, fetched the warm eggs from the coop, and tied the cow out to pasture at the break of dawn. Then fall had come with its wetness, its decaying leaves. Then winter with its snow, falling on her father's grave underneath a cherry tree in a cemetery overgrown with weeds and cobwebs. The years had passed by, and when Galina was old enough, she had moved to Kiev, where she met Umaru, a Nigerian student studying international politics at the university. It hadn't been long before they married and moved to Nigeria, into an old colonial house and into a life of leisure, of expats, of cultural coagulation that would result only in heartbreak.

In the car, the thought of her past, which was still a fresh wound, caused Galina's heart to beat faster. She gripped the steering wheel tighter and accelerated into the path of a swallow. The bird catapulted upward and landed on the road in front of her.

"Shit." Galina stopped the car. As she opened the door, she thought this moment to be an ominous sign. She couldn't tell if the bird was merely stunned or dead. It was lying on its side; its wings were unusually large, and the soft brownish feathers beneath its head were dotted with four white spots. It was dead. Galina cupped the bird in her hand and placed it in the tall grass by the side of the road.

"I killed a swallow." That was the first thing she said when she got to her mother's house.

"But you are here, my dearest daughter! That is all that matters to me." Her mother threw open her arms and kissed her tightly. "Besides, we can drink some of that bad omen away," she continued, winking in the direction of a small shed.

"You've been making vodka?" Galina asked.

"How else do you expect me to make a little money, or return a favor? Uncle Ivan came by yesterday to help me harvest some wheat. He took home a jar of my vodka. Let's go inside," her mother said, and she led the way, walking slowly toward the kitchen by an orchard of pear and apple trees overburdened with ripening fruit.

AFTER THE LUNCH of borscht her mother prepared, Galina returned to Drabov, where she had rented a small, barely furnished one-bedroom apartment. As soon as she unlocked the door, she ran the bath—and then she flung off her clothes, shoving them into a plastic bag. Later in the evening, she would do what she always did when she returned from her visits to her mother: she would soak the clothes in hot water overnight and then wash them by hand. She was walking around her apartment in just her underwear when the phone rang.

"Hello? Hello?"

She immediately knew who the shouting voice was. It was Umaru, calling from Nigeria. She pictured his face, always open and inviting, and the way he often furrowed his brow when he spoke, his tall body, attractive and lean, and then she fought the impulse to hang up.

"Yes?" Her English sounded foreign to her ears.

"Galina, Galina—can you hear me?"

"What do you want? How did you find me?"

"I'm calling to say I'm—"

She gave in to the impulse and hung up.

By the time she reached the bathroom and opened the door, the phone rang again. Galina stepped into the narrow room and shut the door behind her, leaning against the door, her back in knots, her arms heavy and hands in fists. She caught her reflection in the small mirror above the dripping sink, and she felt a whoosh of air leave her thin lips. The face that stared back at her was as pale as the moon, and because her pupils were dilated in her large eyes, she thought again about how she resembled a bird. She unclenched her fists and touched her chin, where sunspots had emerged, reminding her of those sunny days in Nigeria when she had changed into her bikini, thrown a towel on the grass outside their house, and taken in the hot rays of the equatorial sun. One such day she had felt a nudge on her right shoulder, and found a Nigerian neighbor standing over her.

"Madam, madam, are you okay?" he had said.

She had removed her sunglasses and laughed out loud. "Yes, of course. I'm just sunbathing."

He had nodded and walked away quickly as if embarrassed.

In the bathroom Galina laughed to herself—a contrived laugh, at once girlish and manic. If she was losing her mind, this might be one of the symptoms. But she was unlikely to do the research required to know what happens to a person when her internal world suffers a sudden obliteration or collapse. No, there was no need for any research; she was here to begin anew.

The phone rang again.

Galina undressed fully and slipped into the bath, sinking into its warmth, deeper and deeper until more than half her head was submerged and she couldn't hear the ringing of the phone. Until all was silent like in a dream.

ONE WEEK LATER, Galina drove back to the exclusion zone to visit her mother. She was leaving a trail of voicemail messages from Olexa behind her. The first one, in his calm, deep, unaffected voice: "Where are you?" The second one: "Are you around?" And the third and fourth one, again: "Where are you?"

Her mind had begun to repress everything and anything that reminded her of the past, especially those moments that occurred in sequence. One. Two. Three. Four. The number of times she had miscarried her babies. The number of times she had failed to give Umaru a son—or a daughter. The number of times Umaru's mother had arrived from her village near Kano only to say, "Ah-ah, not yet? Not even one? How come?" What was the word her Nigerian doctor had used to describe her condition? Yes, *barren*. She was a barren woman.

In her car, Galina followed a winding tarred road through a land so fertile it was hard to believe. Nature had taken over, giving rise to a dense tangle of trees and vegetation in areas where people had once lived, and allowing for a surge in the population of animals. The last time she traveled this road, she had spotted a wild boar moving swiftly by the edge of the forest. She had once imagined that in Nigeria she would be living alongside jungles filled with lions and cobras. It occurred to her that she had never seen a lion in the wild in all the years she lived in northern Nigeria, where the land, flat and dry, stretched far into a horizon dotted with shrubs, the occasional tree, and rocks. Nor had she ever seen a cobra. The only snake she ever saw was a puff adder, which Umaru had found and killed in their garage.

She slowed down at the checkpoint and smiled warmly at the guards. Reaching into her handbag, she pulled out two packets of cigarettes.

"Here." She offered them to one of the guards.

"Well, thank you," he said.

The other one cleared his throat. "We've been informed that an old woman died a few hours ago in one of the villages. We won't know who until she's been identified, but we are following orders and telling folks who are coming through now."

The image of the dead swallow filled Galina's mind. "My mother?"

"We don't know, you hear?"

She nodded, her head bobbing as if detached, and she drove off, raising radioactive dust in her wake.

Galina came upon field after field after passing Shramkovka, each one a reminder of how much distance she had to cover to get to her mother's house. Visions came. More birds. Not swallows but vultures this time, with dusty light-brown feathers and balding heads that were too small for their bodies. In the fields behind their house in Nigeria, the vultures had landed often, hovering excitedly over some poor dead thing.

"Enough," she said out loud to herself. She pressed her right foot down on the accelerator, lurching forward over the forsaken and fertile land.

When she got to her mother's house, the ducklings her mother kept were in a delirious state. They had not been fed. They followed her, staying close to her heels, quacking mercilessly. Her mother was not there. Not in the kitchen. Not in the main house, where an old radio played a merry folk song.

She had been planning to tell her mother why she had returned to the country. In time. She would tell her Umaru's secret: He had taken another wife in his village and impregnated her. Galina returned to the kitchen and observed the beginnings of a pot of borscht that her mother had started: half a head of cabbage, shredded carrots and beets, a handful of dill hastily harvested, large beans in a white metal cup, and no potatoes.

A thud on the kitchen window caused Galina to jump back. When she peered beyond the windowsill covered with unripe heirloom tomatoes and dead flies and onto the ground below, she caught sight of the swallow that had just flown into the glass. It had fallen by a gooseberry bush and stood immobile, stunned. Galina turned away from the window and walked out into the yard where the ducklings accosted her again. They followed her as she made her way to the wide sloping garden behind her mother's house, along the narrow path lined with sunflowers on one side and vegetables on the other, and toward a small pond covered with duckweed. The ducklings entered the pond, and Galina watched as their small orange beaks dove into the water, searching for sustenance.

If she hadn't taken her favorite path back and wandered as she had done as a child, through the orchard where a carpet of rotten apples and pears crunched beneath her feet, over the sturdy mound of the underground cellar emerging out of the ground like a grave, she probably would never have heard her mother's voice, muffled and distant, coming from the open rusted pipe above the mound.

"Galina!"

And that was how she found her mother, not dead but six feet underground in the cellar, where she had gone to get potatoes for borscht and fallen, twisting her ankle.

AFTER THREE DAYS, when the swelling in her ankle had gone down, Galina's mother ordered Galina back to work.

"Go. I will be fine. Besides, you promised to come visit again this weekend." Her mother was perched comfortably on a divan by a window that overlooked a walnut tree, its branches hanging low with green fruit.

Since she had found her mother in the cellar, something in Galina's being had shifted and a feeling of euphoria had crept in. She flitted around the house, her arms light and reaching, for the rugs on the floor that needed dusting, for the empty water bucket, for the knob on the old television, for a bowl of borscht that she placed by her mother's bed, for apples in the orchard that she also placed by her mother's bed, and finally for her mother's face, which she held close to her own and kissed goodbye.

She got into her car and drove toward home, and as soon as she passed the guards at the checkpoint, she remembered a childhood song. It was short and sweet, and the words rolled off her tongue like soft clouds. The first line, sung underneath gray skies: *May there always be blue skies.* On either side of her, large evergreens grew thick inside a darkening forest. The second line: *May there always be sunshine.* The sun hid behind clouds. The third line: *May there always be Mother.* Galina's eyes filled with tears and she found herself laughing into the fourth line: *May there always be me.* The end to an odd sequence, to a song she had learned in Soviet youth camp. She repeated the words, and again her tears and laughter occurred together.

The city of Drabov also lay underneath gray skies. In front of her apartment building, Galina parked her car by a small playground filled with children wearing colorful clothes. With a quick wave, she greeted the old women sitting on a wooden bench by a sandbox, and then she walked into the dim musty hallway of the building. Because she felt lucky and happy that day, she took the old elevator, which banged shut and rattled loudly as it journeyed to the fourth floor. She had just emerged from the elevator and was unlocking her door when she heard the phone ringing. Like a bird she alighted toward the telephone and picked up the receiver, and without much of a pause said, "I am here," for she was sure it was Olexa.

But the voice on the phone was not Olexa's. It was Uncle Ivan's.

"I'm sorry, Galochka."

Galina's arms grew heavy. She cleared her throat, but her lips emitted almost no sound.

"I just found your mother on the divan—she's dead."

All Galina heard, through an open window in the kitchen, were the peals of laughter coming from the playground outside.

Angela Ajayi's essays, book reviews, and author interviews have appeared in *The Common* online, *Wild River Review*, *Star Tribune*, and *Afroeuropa: Journal of Afroeuropean Studies*. She spent more than ten years in publishing, mainly as a book editor at Africa World Press/The Red Sea Press. She holds a BA in English literature from Calvin College and an MA in comparative literature from Columbia University. Recently she was selected for the 2016–2017 Loft Mentor Series in fiction. Nigerian and Ukrainian by birth and American by citizenship, she lives in Minneapolis with her husband and daughter.

EDITOR'S NOTE

From the first paragraph of Laura Chow Reeve's "1,000-Year-Old Ghosts," I knew this story was something special. I was immediately intrigued by the attention to the sensory details involved in the act of pickling memories and the odd but confident way Reeve treated memories as something physical. What followed was a beautiful, magical story about three generations of women wrestling with their painful memories. The story is deceivingly simple, despite its fabulist qualities and poetic prose, and yet it moves deeply. The transformation of memories—both a blessing and a burden—into something physical and malleable allows the story to leap beyond the familiar philosophical questions of their importance. Instead, it highlights how many immigrants and those descended from them wrestle with the paradox of both wanting to hold on to the experiences that have made them, and wanting to forget the pain that these memories have caused.

"1,000-Year-Old Ghosts" exemplifies what we're looking for when we select fiction—lyrical writing, inventiveness of plot, a point of view touched by the Asian American experience, and; most important, a story infused with deep empathy and heart.

Karissa Chen, editor in chief
Hyphen

1,000-YEAR-OLD GHOSTS

Laura Chow Reeve

POPO TAUGHT ME to pickle memories when I was thirteen. It's just like cucumbers, radishes, cabbage. I learned to cut them into even squares. Memories cut like apples; the knife slides through their protective skin with a crisp snap. I packed them in jars filled with salt, sugar, vinegar, and water. No herbs and spices because they can distort the memories, make them seem too sweet or too bitter.

"It's a family secret," she said to me. "It allows you to forget."

"Forget what?" I asked.

"Anything. Forgetting does not come easily to the women in our family. We have our jars."

"What are we trying to forget, Popo?"

"So many questions. Chop this into smaller pieces."

We started with minor moments: (1) When I dropped my underwear on the floor of the changing room after swim practice at school and Abigail Kincaid picked it up and showed the whole class. (2) The time I tugged on a strange woman's skirt in a Costco checkout line because I thought, for a second, that she was my mother. (3) A recurring nightmare of being alone in an abandoned building with no way to get out.

"How do you feel?" she asked after the first lids were tightened.

It felt like clenching and unclenching my jaw, like a steady beat of tension and release. It felt like being full and empty at the same time. Instead of telling her this, I shrugged.

She never asks him about a future where he does not come back. When she is alone, she prays that he will return to her. She asks him what he would like for dinner. Before they go to bed, she prays that business will stay good. Their silence is steady and it endures. It is a silence they have agreed to.

He travels back and forth between their apartment in San Francisco and southern China. It is rare to have a husband whose body tastes like the Pacific Ocean. It is rare to have a husband made mostly of salt.

I WAS POPO'S daughter's daughter, but our saltwater bond was stronger than blood. We exhausted my mother.

"Ma, why are you teaching her that?" she asked. It was a gray Sunday morning and Popo was helping me pickle a few things. It had been a bad week.

"Because you won't," Popo said.

"Do you have your own jars, Mom?" I asked. I had searched for them without any luck.

"No," she said. Like Popo, my mother was good at shutting down conversations. There were so many times that she felt far away. My arms could never quite reach her.

"That's not true, Anne," Popo said. "We made you one or two when you were younger. You remember that."

"Is that right?" Mom wasn't looking at either of us. She was still holding a paper napkin she had used at breakfast. She was trying to smooth out the creases with her fingers.

"Yes," Popo said.

"I'm sick of this." My mother's fingers tore the napkin to pieces. "How come you decide what all of us remember or forget?" There was water in her eyes.

I wanted to wipe it away for her, but I was afraid her tears would not be like mine. I was afraid my mother was not made of salt.

"You know what, Ma?" my mother said. "I remember everything."

The street outside their apartment is loud the way city streets tend to be. The sound drifts in through the open windows of their front room, and she lets it fill up the space he left behind. It sits in his favorite chair, the blue one next to the fireplace. After it is well rested, it moves across the front room and embeds itself into the cracks in the floorboards. It touches all of his books and then settles into his side of the bed. She holds it as she falls asleep. She smells it the next morning in her hair. She keeps it there until the rest of the city wakes up and it makes its way outside again.

When he comes home, he shuts the windows and says he is tired of loud noises. He tells her how the ocean roars and the wind cracks. He tells her he has been looking forward to the silence of home.

MY MOTHER WENT through my room to find my jars and display them on the kitchen counter. They would confront me when I got home from school. One day, after she had found five of them tucked in my sock drawer, my mother told me to sit down with her.

"I know Popo thinks this is best, but memories are important even when they are painful. I'm concerned about you," she said. "Both of you."

"I'm fine, Mom. Popo is fine," I said.

"She's not fine. Her short-term memory is getting worse. She forgets where she puts things, she doesn't show up to appointments, she can't even tell me what she had for breakfast some days. Popo isn't fine." Her voice was clear and calm, but it bounced inside my head until it ached.

I looked at my jars on the kitchen counter and tried to remember what was in them. They could have been anyone's jars. The liquid inside was murky, almost gray. I wanted to open them up. I wanted to push them off the ledge to see them break open.

"Do you really remember everything?" I asked her. I tried to remember stories about her before she had me, ones that she must have told me, but I couldn't find any.

"Nobody remembers everything," she said.

"But you told Popo—"

"I was upset."

"Tell me what you remember then."

We stayed at the kitchen table and she talked. The darkness slipped into the room and sat down with us. I couldn't see my mother's gaze through the dark—we hadn't turned the lights on— but I could feel it on my skin.

Things she told me: Popo would prepare for Gung Gung's home- comings with his favorite dishes—winter melon soup and salted duck. Popo would wear a pink dress on those days because she said Gung Gung was tired of the blues and greens of the ocean. Popo's comforter was white and felt like velvet, even though it was only made of cotton. Popo would let my mother sleep with her when

Gung Gung was away. My mother met my father when they both worked for an insurance company in downtown Sacramento. They were both already married, but my father asked my mother out for a drink one day after work and she said yes. Popo liked my father because he was really American, unlike my mother's first husband, who grew up in Chinatown like them. My parents loved each other so much that she was never hungry. When my father left without saying goodbye, my mother ate everything in the refrigerator and the pantry and the cupboards.

The memories came in pieces. Sometimes she stumbled, searched for something else to tell me. She wanted to fill the silence but didn't have enough words. When she was done, she asked me how I felt, and I didn't have the heart to tell her that it felt the same. It felt like clenching and unclenching my jaw, like a steady beat of tension and release. I felt full and empty at the same time.

She is less lonely now that she has Anne. She has something to hold on to when she walks through Chinatown, something to ground her to the sidewalk. She used to think that she would float away. Now she walks with purpose.

She teaches Anne how to say apple *and* block *in English. She does not talk to her in Cantonese. When she does not know the word she is looking for in English she says nothing.*

As I GOT older, I filled my jars and it was a feeling larger than relief. I poured out jams, mayonnaise, and peanut butter. I clogged every drain in the house to create a space to put myself away.

(1) The song that was playing when I lost my virginity to a

boy who changed the sheets right after. (2) The white woman at the grocery store who told me I was prettier because I wasn't full Chinese. Her hands in my hair: "You're so lucky," she said. (3) The men who leered at me when I walked down the street and the one who told me, "I've never had one like you before." (4) How my mother looked after the spindled cancer cells settled into her body. (5) The woman on the bus who spoke to me in Cantonese, and how I did not know how to respond. I searched for words that someone should have taught me, and I couldn't find them anywhere.

Popo never warned me not to let it become a habit, a practice, a daily ritual. Mom wasn't around to count my jars, display them, remind me of things I had already forgotten, witness my slow dissolve. I made the pickling liquid in large batches. I bought sugar and vinegar in bulk. My jars overflowed and spilled onto my hands until they stung.

Every time he comes back, he feels more foreign. He says, "Néih hóu ma," but she responds in English. She practices with Anne. She learns new words every day.

"One day Anne's children will not know how to speak our language," he tells her.

She wants to say, "Maybe that will be for the best. They will stop longing for things they cannot have. There will be no reason to leave. Not everyone can live in between things. Not everyone can survive being split into two. There are fish that die in saltwater."

✦

POPO DRANK A glass of saltwater every night before her evening prayers. One night I asked why, and she said it was a leftover habit from when my Gung Gung would travel. "He died on his way back to China. Did you know that?"

"You told me," I said.

"I just wanted to make sure you didn't forget."

She poured salt into the bottom of an empty glass and then filled the glass with water at the kitchen sink. She took her time, drank it while she was reading a magazine. I had never asked for a glass and she had never offered.

"Popo?" I asked after her glass was washed and set down to dry. "What do you put in your jars?"

"I don't remember," she said. "That is their purpose."

"But aren't there things you wish you hadn't forgotten?" I asked.

She looked at me for a long time before she answered. "No," she said.

Then she added in a softer voice, "Sometimes I think there are not enough jars in this city for me to fill."

He is dying but refuses to die in America. "I am going home," he says. "I cannot be buried here." He makes the necessary travel arrangements. He plans to leave in only a few weeks.

"You are leaving me here," she says to him.

"Yes."

"What am I supposed to do without you?" she asks. "What about Anne?"

"What does it matter? I am dying either way." He looks at her and smiles. "You don't want my ghost to haunt you. It's better for both of us if I go."

"Yes," she says. "You're right."

To guarantee that she is not haunted by her dead husband, she stuffs most of what she has of him into thirty-seven glass jars. She leaves only enough to tell her future grandchildren (1) his name (2) his occupation (3) where he was born (4) where he died (5) the saltiness of his breath.

She does not have a backyard to bury the jars, so she pushes him underneath her bed instead. The first night that she sleeps with them, she hears a steady humming that keeps her awake. It never goes away, and she never moves the jars. Instead, she learns to live with the hum until she forgets it is even there.

"ANNE, GRAB ME the measuring cups," she said one afternoon.

"Popo," I said. "I'm Katie. Anne was my mother."

Her eyebrows furrowed. She moved around me and grabbed the measuring cups for herself.

"Please stop. This is making you sick," I said.

She continued to measure and chop; she licked her index finger, dipped it into a bowl of salt in front of her, and then popped it back in her mouth to taste.

I wanted to imitate her, feel the small grains on my own tongue, but I stopped myself.

"I'm close," she said.

"Close to what? What else could you have to forget?" I slammed my hands on the counter. Her bowl of salt shook.

We stood in silence until she said, "I love you, but I wish I remembered how to say it the other way."

"What do you mean?" I asked.

The tears on her face looked almost milky white.

"There was a way I used to say it. I don't remember the words. I used to say it to someone," she said. "Do you remember?"

"No, Popo," I said. "I don't."

When she takes care of Katie, she does not put her down. Katie's skin is soft underneath her fingertips and she wonders how much sadness this little body can take. She smells just like Anne did when she was a baby, but looks so different. There are only traces of Anne and it makes Katie harder to hold on to. She is half-ghost. If she puts Katie down, she will disappear, and she will not be able to find her again. She holds on to her because this is not a thing she can let go of.

BY THE END, her pickling process had picked up speed. Everything I loved became smaller and smaller until she started to break apart in my hands and fall through my permanently wrinkled fingertips. Seven years after my mom died, she finished dissolving.

My memory was shaky. Most of the water in my body was salt. I no longer had difficulty forgetting; it came easily with or without a jar. Remembering was harder.

As I packed up her home, I looked for all the places that Popo had put herself to rest. I walked through each room, sat on each chair, picked up each knickknack, ran my fingers over every book's spine. I went through all of her drawers, her closets. I took every lid off every box. Jars were hidden everywhere.

She was right. There hadn't been enough jars in the city to hold everything she needed to put away. She had started to fill milk jugs and ice cream pints. Even her shampoo bottles and toothpaste tubes had memories stuffed inside them.

I laid them out in her living room. They took up every inch of the floor. I balanced them on top of each other. They sank between couch cushions. One or two rolled behind the television. I played a childhood game to choose one: *My mother said to pick the very best one and that is—*

Like the others, its contents blurred in the murky liquid. I wanted to say that it looked familiar, but of course it didn't. I pulled on the lid, but my hands kept slipping. I was too weak, or the jar was too strong, or whatever was inside didn't want to be taken back.

I threw it against the wall. The glass shattered, the liquid dripped to the floor, and the memory clung to the paint. Its smell surprised me—orange peels and baby powder. Popo was holding my mother's head in her lap, pushing her hair back with her hands, cooing to her softly. The memory played in a loop, but each time something was slightly different. Sometimes Popo's shirt was a different color; sometimes my mother's head rested on her shoulder; sometimes my mother looked older or younger. I couldn't pick it up entirely; it kept slipping out of my hands.

One by one, I opened the rest of them. Some smelled rancid, like death. These were ones of her travels from China, her first few years living in San Francisco, my mother's sickness and funeral. Many smelled like the ocean, like Gung Gung's seawater breath, like the smells that made up her heartbreak. The ones of me smelled like vanilla yogurt and strawberries.

The floor was wet. I lay down in the mess and let my clothes soak it all up. If my mother and Popo had been there, I would have told them this: (1) I still long for things I cannot have. (2) I am not split in two, but I am still living between things. (3) We are drowning in all this saltwater.

Laura Chow Reeve is a writer living in Jacksonville, Florida. She has an MA in Asian American Studies from UCLA and a BA from Bryn Mawr College. She is a VONA alumna.

EDITOR'S NOTE

Ben Shattuck's "Edwin Chase of Nantucket" was originally selected by our guest editor, Paul Harding, who described it as having captured "that weather-swept island and the souls who lived on it" in the late eighteenth century. What we love about this piece is the way it conjures the isolation and remoteness of island life, a world of birds, sea, sky, and salt marsh, sealed off from the rest of the world. Shattuck's islanders are people who live with little and yet make much of what they have. He captures at once the richness—"of quinces, apples, dried cherries, pears, a side of dried venison"; "the smell of rain like wet stone, and of the marsh. Bits of quahogs and seaweed spread over the sandbar, which would soon sink under the incoming tide"—and the deprivation of island life in a period quite remote from our own. At once sweet and salty, it is a lyrical, evocative story, a bit mysterious, strange and yet strangely familiar, as all the very best stories are.

Christina Thompson, editor
Harvard Review

EDWIN CHASE OF NANTUCKET

Ben Shattuck

WHEN MY FATHER and I were younger, he taught me how to count the days in a month. Put your fists up like this, he said, side by side. January is the first knuckle, the peak. February, the valley. The peak has more days. The valley, less. January has thirty-one. February, twenty-eight. And so on. Down to double-knuckled summer. I must have been ten or eleven when he showed me that, a few years after we'd moved to Nantucket. I lay in bed that night, searching for other timepieces. I touched twenty-four ribs. The daily hours. Eyes, nostrils, mouth, and ears that made seven. The week. There might be moon phases down my spine; days between the equinox and solstice somewhere in my feet. I could be made of three hundred and sixty-five bones.

May is a knuckle. I know that without counting because on the thirty-first, 1796, a man and a young pregnant woman—carrying between them nothing but a satchel of clothes, two sketchbooks, bottles of turpentine, paints, and brushes—arrived unexpectedly to our farm on Coskata. I was twenty when they came.

It had been raining all morning. Puddles held in sand. Winter had been long, April ended in a blizzard, and snow still lay in ditches and in the house's shadow. So much of my day then was shaped by the sky—the way a cloud gathered itself up and fell in rain or snow or sleet. Nantucket starts and ends with weather. Which way the wind was blowing and why. What clouds meant.

This was over a year since Dad died. He had left in the morning to cut ice from the Pinkhams' pond. The blocks he carted home sometimes held duck feathers, hairs of green winter growth, a brown and bent rush. As if the ice were inscribing itself with feathers and stems. The evening he disappeared, I found his coat folded in the grass beside the pond. I took it home, told my mother, Laurel, that he'd probably gone on one of his walks, and then we went to bed. It wasn't until I crossed the pond the next day that I found him, out in the center, facedown, under the ice. His shirt had ridden up over his head, so that when I stood over him it seemed that wind was blowing across his back, or that he was undressing. One shoe was missing. I retrieved the saw. Cut him out. His gray hair was thick with ice. The skin on his face looked tauter. So much was still there, but more missing: his deep voice; his quietness; his limp from the leg broken twice over in the war. I sat on the ice with him for most of the evening before bringing him home on Sadie's back. I couldn't figure out how he'd gotten all the way out to there and under the ice.

When Will and Rivkah came—though I didn't know their names then—Laurel and I were by the shed rubbing oil on Sadie. Her fleas had been bad that winter. I should have kept her stall cleaner. Before fleas it was thrush—the bottoms of her hooves smothered with white rot. All horses' maladies are poetry, Dad said, like bog spavin or seedy toe. Our old horse, Julius, had moon blindness. Both corneas dyed milk-blue. We led him through the dunes and along the beach for exercise on our evening walks because he was scared into laziness by his cloudy eyes.

Sadie stepped back and turned her head when she saw them.

That's the way it always is—an animal noticing first. Gulls crowd in the sheep pasture before a gale; songbirds fly into the chimney. I try to think of the day before they came—if our cow was giving bad milk.

They were in the middle of the sand road that nobody used. We were ten miles to Nantucket town, and the only building beyond our house was the lighthouse, a mile away at the end of the point. Nobody came to our house. The only prints on the path were made by me, Laurel, mice, and the birds. The punctuation of our solitude—commas and periods in the footsteps of animals, the pauses between us and town.

"Who's that?" I said to Laurel.

"What?" she said, looking up at me. She used the back of her wrist to brush her hair from her forehead. Oil dripped from her fingers.

She was thirty-seven then. That makes her seventeen when I was born. My father had been much older—somewhere in his late thirties. The bones in her face were severe in a way that might have been ugly. A straight nose, thin lips, narrow face, deep eye sockets. But it happened that everything was placed well, beautifully even, and she could easily have remarried if we weren't all those miles from town. Two suitors did ride to our farm. One was John Throat, the butcher, whom I met twice a year at the end of Coatue. He came for Laurel cleaner than usual, with a bundle of meat tied to his horse. My mother was polite, fixed him tea, and then asked him to leave. Since then, each time I walk a hog down Coatue to meet him, neither of us mentions his visit. The other suitor was Uncle Amos, who stayed for two nights in the upstairs storage room. On the third day he told us at breakfast that he'd been mistaken in coming, apologized, and left. I haven't seen him since.

"Behind you," I said to her then. "Down the road."

She turned.

"Oh," she said, stepping back. "Yes." She touched her hairline. "Or—no."

"What?"

"I thought it was—but no, there are two. So I suppose not."

"Suppose not what?"

"Nothing," she said. "It's not Paul?" She turned back to Sadie, and poured another ladleful of oil. "And Maggie?"

Paul Pinkham was the keeper of the Great Point Lighthouse, that mile north. He lived there with his mute wife, Sarah, and their daughter, Maggie—a few years older than I and to whom I was engaged. Paul had white hair and a beard bigger than his head that you could see from a long way off. And he wouldn't have been walking like that, the way these two were separated.

"No," I said. "And that's not Maggie behind him."

Laurel turned again. Put her hand up to her forehead to block the sun.

"I don't know, Edwin. I guess we just have to wait and see."

In those minutes of watching the two hobble forward through the wet sand, there were the sounds of gulls screeching, of the wind passing over our house and the dune grass, and of the sea feeling the land, saying to it with each wave, *Here you are, here you are, here you are.*

OUR HOUSE WAS a sacrifice to the wind. The wind rattled the fireboards and casements at night. The wind threw sand on the windows and guided it through the siding, no matter how many times I resealed it. Sand came down the chimney. Pooled on the hearthstone. Snaked over the floorboards. Banked up on all sides of the house. Collected at the feet of the table. It came in on my clothes, in my hair, under my fingernails, and filled my bed. I dug it out of my eyes before I fell asleep. My shoes were shovels. I swept the house every day, and still. "At least we won't need to dig the graves," Laurel would say, "when we're buried here."

Dad left us for the war from 1780 through 1783, when I was seven. He came home more wordless, disappeared for long walks, swept the house in the middle of the night, talked to himself. He pried up floorboards by the chimney and front door and put hexes under them—one of his shoes by the chimney, an eel spear by the door. He took off his hair, eyebrows, and eyelashes one morning shave. Laurel drew on eyebrows with charcoal. Then there was the pond. Then me and Laurel living alone beside the Pinkhams. Then me, every summer, mucking out marsh mud to better the soil in the hotbeds for our vegetables, loading the ground with seeds, and scything marsh hay and piling it on the staddles. Me, asking Laurel if she was sick, and her saying "It's nothing." My life then was comfortable, I think. Secure. I would have enough tea for a few cups a day. I would marry Maggie. I would see John Throat a few times a year. I would help Paul Pinkham paint the lighthouse every few years. My mother might get sicker, though maybe not. My father would continue to not come back from the pond. Sadie would get fleas again. The sheep would lamb. The seals would continue to stare at us from the waves. This might last another sixty years.

·

I SAW THAT Will, almost at the fence, held his boots. Plodding through the sand. On his shoulder it looked like he was carrying a small, dark sack. A cat. A brown cat with its tail crossing his neck.

"Should I get the gun?" I asked Laurel.

She was breathing hard. She smiled to herself. Coughed.

"No. I know who it is."

She untied her apron, wiped her hands, and draped it over her shoulder. She tucked her hair behind her ears. That was a habit of hers— always touching her hair, brushing her fingers across her forehead.

The cat's tail batted Will's chest. He opened the gate, walked through, dropped his boots, shrugged off his satchel.

"Jesus," he said. "You live at the end of the world. My legs feel like they've been beaten."

He lifted the cat from his shoulder, and put it on the sand. "I was going to quit three miles back." He waved behind himself, toward Rivkah. "But I was too thirsty."

He smiled, cocked his head to the side. "Hello, Laurel."

I stepped around Sadie.

"Look what I found," he said, pointing to the cat rubbing itself on my mother's leg. "For you. Whatever's the opposite of a welcome gift. She's that."

"You're here," Laurel said, folding her arms.

"I am," he said. He threw his arms up. "Sorry."

She stepped forward and hugged him. He shelved his head on her shoulder. They parted.

"This is Edwin?" he said, looking at me.

Sadie shifted, and I avoided her hooves.

"Yes," Laurel said. "Edwin, this is Will."

He squinted. Blond hair. A thin beard. Blue eyes. He smiled, and long, crescent dimples appeared.

"I haven't seen you since you were this big," he said. He sank his palm close to the ground.

"Three," Laurel said.

"Is that so?" he said. "You look like your mother. More than your father."

"Who are you?" I asked.

Will looked at Laurel, and when she didn't say anything, he said, "A friend of your mother's."

Laurel touched her hairline. "Yes," she said.

The gate clapped shut. We all turned.

"Finally," Will said.

Rivkah's pregnancy came first. Her dress swept over her legs. Her coat parted over her stomach. Her steps were heavy and short.

"Who?" Laurel said.

"Rivkah Seixas," Will said.

She didn't come to us, but sat in the sand by the fence. She touched her stomach.

"Not what you think," Will said. "Or who you think. Not mine."

Long, black hair covered her face and shoulders like the wing of a great bird.

"Who is she?" Laurel asked.

"She's from Newport," Will said. "A patron's daughter. I'll explain later."

Rivkah put her elbows on her knees. She was heaving.

"Is she sick?" Laurel said.

"Just tired, I imagine," Will said. "From the long march."

"Why didn't you get her a carriage from town?" Laurel said.

"Why did Silas build a farm about near Portugal?" he said.

I hadn't heard my father's name spoken aloud since Paul Pinkham would come around the house asking for him. With my mother, it was "your father." To hear it was like seeing him suddenly.

"You're from Newport?" I asked.

"Edwin," Laurel said, "could you get some water for the girl?"

"No," Will said. "She's from Newport. I was painting her family portrait last fall. She found me as I was on my way here. I'm sorry, Laurel."

She hesitated. "I'm glad you're here," she finally said.

"Good," Will said. He put a hand on my shoulder. "Any food with that water? We haven't eaten in some time."

"Of course we do," Laurel said.

"Or, if you have milk," he said, "that would be better."

When the English occupied the island, they first stole our sheep. Laurel was afraid they'd take more from the house, and so one day she and I went out beside the marsh and buried our silverware, dishware, and the little paper money we had. I felt like gathering everything up and burying it then, when I walked inside for water. Like going to my room for the poetry books, into the kitchen for the pans. The two chairs angled toward each other by the fire where Laurel and I sat every night.

I filled two cups from a jug of our cow's milk, went outside, and put one in the sand beside Rivkah.

She didn't look up. Her thumbs were making circles over blisters on the tops of her feet. Embarrassed, I turned away. Yellow puffs of wood dust were falling from the edge of the barn roof. One of the carpenter wasps kicked away sawdust as it dug farther. They were everywhere that spring. Digging hundreds of round holes in the barn and house, and I didn't know how to get rid of them. Laurel had suggested smoking them out. I'd nearly burned the barn down when I held flaming grass under the roof line.

"Thanks," Will said when I handed him his cup, and gulped down the milk that our cow had made from dead grass.

"Darling," Laurel said. "Why don't you get us a duck? I've seen teals landing in the marsh all week."

"Duck," Will said, handing the cup back to me. "That would be something. I haven't had one in some time." His hand wandered over Sadie's ears.

My job was simple then: introduce a ram, double the heartbeats every year, then reduce. That might be the story of the living. Pull a fish from the sea. Take milk from a cow. Cut peat from the ground. Shoot a duck from the sky. Take a little bit of everything from everywhere. At the end of the year I'd pray I'd added more than all we'd taken to stay alive. In the winter, if a late flock of geese landed on the pond, I shot as many as I could and kept them frozen on the laundry lines between the shed and house.

Rivkah still hadn't moved. I stepped between the two fresh sets of footprints, going the other way.

MALLARDS SLID ACROSS the black-watered marsh. An egret's oversize wings gulped air across the grass. Laurel's teals were rafted by the far edge, just below the small windmill of the saltworks, the drying vats of which I'd covered in the past week because of the storms. Coots, buffleheads, and redheads landed on the sandbar. More circling overhead.

I sat in the grass, waiting for one to paddle close enough so that I wouldn't waste a shot. Toward Wauwinet, two hay staddles stood like wardens over the marsh. Paul's dog barked in the distance.

Weather painted the horizon. There was the smell of rain like wet stone, and of the marsh. Bits of quahogs and seaweed spread over the sandbar, which would soon sink under the incoming tide. This could be the day that the tide didn't stop, when it washed through the spartina, lifted and toppled the cut hay from the staddles, when it crept through the bayberry, pushed wavelets onto the dunes, touched our floor, mixed our fire's ashes, rose through the chimney, and over our house. One hurricane, I saw an upright barn float lazily through the marsh, hay paying out from its loft.

I put my gun under my knees and tented my body with my jacket as the rain began to fall.

There had been unexpected arrivals in the past. After the war, packs of dogs roamed the island looking for food. That was one bounty, for dogs' heads. Then there was the half-wit who lived in the dunes for a week, until my father walked him to town. There was Maggie's former husband, whom I'd seen walking past our house, near running past our house, to, I found out later, try to talk her into moving back in with him. There was the shipwreck carrying horses down at Great Point. The captain, gun in hand, sat in the sand, beside two dead horses with broken legs. Paul had put a blanket over him. At least I could figure out the scene when I came upon it. The storm, the man, the gun, broken legs, the dead horses. Cause, effect, and the blanket to finish it.

Nothing like this, though. Nobody either of us knew.

I looked up, and there was a duck, right overhead. When I shot, it folded from the sky and slapped the water beside me. I was an animal then, I suppose, smelling the wind, logging details. The tide. The arrangement of ducks on the water. The grasses. The weather. I cut the bird's neck and started home by way of the beach. A dead animal's heat makes me uneasy.

I stood in the sand to watch the wind draw a thread of shorebirds between waves. Everyone was migrating. Soon it'd be summer, and then winter. And then a year would have passed. In the pond, a swan struggled to lift into flight, leaving a long white track. I cut handfuls of rushes from the shore.

✦

THE RAIN HAD passed, and the clouds over the house looked like pieces of the sun. Sparks washed out the chimney.

When I passed through the gate, I saw Rivkah in my bedroom window, bent beside a candle on the windowsill. When she saw me, she lifted the candle from the windowsill and sank back into the room. I went around to the peat shed and tucked a few bricks under my arm.

Laurel's feet were in Will's lap when I opened the door. There they were by the fire, she in her chair, he in mine, which he'd moved so it was opposite hers. A stack of driftwood was violently aflame beside them. She kicked her feet up, sat up straight, and touched her hairline.

Dad had carved a clock into the floorboards just inside the door—an arc of numerals. During the day, the doorframe's shadow kept time on the floor. At night, the numbers were caught useless in the wood.

"The hunter returns!" Will said, reaching down for a bottle of cider on the floor.

"Any luck?" Laurel said. She rose and touched the fire with a poker. Sunlight leaving the wood, my father said of fire.

I held up the duck, shut the door, and then hung my coat on a peg beside Will's satchel.

The cat Will had brought was flattened by the fire, ticking its tail.

"Why are you using the wood?" I said to Laurel, nodding at the fire. In the summer, we used only peat.

She said, "We're celebrating."

"Bit of a chill in the air tonight, isn't there?" Will said. "You'd think the sky was wrung by now."

Laurel picked out a hazelnut from the basket, peeled it, and threw the husk into the fire.

"Was that her upstairs?" I asked.

"Rivkah?" Will said. "Yes. Tired." He cracked a hazelnut with his teeth and spat the shell into his hand. "Bed."

"I thought you could sleep in my room tonight," Laurel said quickly. "For a few nights. Will said he'd sleep in the storeroom."

"With a sack of flour for a pillow," he said.

I filled the kettle and put it to heat on the chimney crane. I put the duck in a pot, twisted its neck so the whole thing fit, and then poured in the water. It braided and parted on the duck's feathers.

When the duck floated, I pushed it down with a spoon.

"If you save some of those nuts, I'll make a cake," I said to Laurel.

"Oh, yes!" Will said. "I hear you're a cook." He reached around his seat and into his coat pocket. "I found these in town," he said, holding out a small pile of peppercorns.

"Thank you," I said to him, and then put the peppercorns in my pocket.

I hung the duck on the chimney crane and singed off the rest of the feathers. A skin of fire stretched over the body.

"What a painting that would make," Will said.

"Are you planning on painting?" Laurel asked.

"Yes. I wanted to make landscapes. I love those huge stacks of salt hay in the marshes. Maybe you can help me, Edwin."

I nodded. Untied the duck, and laid it on the hearthstone.

"Is that what you're doing here?" I said. "Painting?"

"In a way," he said. "And I haven't visited Laurel, well, ever."

My presence had locked some silence over their conversation. Laurel produced stitching. Will went to his satchel for his sketchbook, and with a nub of charcoal from the fireplace began drawing. The only other sound was the occasional creaking of floorboards upstairs.

Cooking is a funeral. Most of the recipes I know I learned from Laurel, before she stopped cooking. The butter and grapes I rubbed on the duck that night was its rite. I wrapped cubes of potato in bacon, stuffed cornmeal into the cavity of the duck. In the kitchen, rosemary, thyme, garlic, hyssop, yellow docks, mint, drying on the ceiling like an inverted, withered garden. On the counter, pickled vegetables, cucumber, beans, beets, and onions. I crushed one peppercorn, and sprinkled it on the duck. I piled the pot with embers, and waited. The smell of the duck filled the room.

"Why is it that you do all the cooking here?" Will said.

Because my father had started lining up his fingernail clippings on the mantel. Because he'd sometimes walk outside without shoes. Because he'd leave me and Laurel alone for hours while he walked. I'd followed him a few times. Mostly he'd just go until he found a spot out of the wind, sit down, and do nothing, miss dinner. She, at first, had gone looking for him. But then, one night, she said to me when I returned from the saltworks, "I don't care what you eat, but I'm not cooking anymore." She put her mother's cookbook for me on the table. She might have a pickled beet for dinner. Or a boiled egg. A handful of nuts.

So I started cooking. In Dad's long disappearances, I improved my recipes. Under the storms battering the house, cooking was the one thing I could control. Everything changes for the better with heat and time: onions go sweet with butter; potatoes soften. Of the raking, mucking, harrowing, it was the hours inside, out of the wind, in the kitchen, where I felt the weight lift away. Under our feet, in the cellar, with blocks of ice from the pond, I kept cheese, a bushel of quinces, apples, dried cherries, pears, a side of dried venison. Turnips and potatoes. And, depending on the season, I put berries into pies: gooseberries, strawberries, meal plums, cranberries, beach plums. When Laurel retreated to the bedroom early, I improved my dessert recipes. I made custards, cranberry tarts, ginger and treacle cakes, pound cakes, bread pudding, and hazelnut cake. I'd leave Dad a plate on the table for when he returned.

"Because I like the warm kitchen," I said to Will then.

"I've never heard of a boy your age spending so much time over the fire," Will said. "But I won't complain."

If cooking is the funeral, eating is its burial. Grace, the eulogy. I served the duck onto three plates. Laurel and I always ate in our chairs by the fire.

"Should I tell Rivkah to come downstairs?" I asked.

"No," Will said. "Let her sleep."

"I'll leave a plate for her," I said.

We sat in silence, eating slowly. Will shifted in his chair, grunted.

"I should tell you—" he said. "I should tell you two about her."

"Tell us if you want," Laurel said. "Some things are best left alone."

He smiled, nodded at her. "Perhaps," he said.

"Paul's wife, Sarah, has delivered babies," she said. "She used to do that in town. She can help. Edwin, you can tell her?"

"Paul?" Will said.

"The lighthouse keeper," Laurel said. She pointed out the window.

Will nodded. "How do you get this thing out?" he said, holding up the bottle and flicking it. His fingernail pinged on the glass. He was referring to the pear in the bottle.

"You have to break it," I said. "But that cider needed another year to mature—I'd like to refill it."

"We'll do everything we can to make her comfortable," Laurel said.

"She'll be fine," Will said.

My father said that every story is a confession if you listen closely enough. Will had done nothing but confess, in some way or another, since he arrived—but somehow I still didn't know him.

EVEN WITHOUT WILL there, Laurel would have stayed up to watch the fire go out, until the logs broke to ash. Sometimes I found her still in her seat by the fire in the morning.

"Good night," I said, after dinner. I packed my pipe and walked into my parents' room.

How familiar, a house. I knew every mark on the floor, the color of each stone of the chimney that I'd stared at for years. But a parent's bed is a private, unknowable thing. I took off only my shoes. I sat up in bed, smoking, watching the ceiling. I heard the poker touching the firedogs as Laurel snuffed the fire. Banking it up, covering it with its own ash to insulate a heart of embers ready to light the next morning. Closing up the night. How long had that fire been going? If we tended it correctly, weeks—the last ember of the night to light the peat of the morning's fire. In the winter, it could be a month before we used the tinderbox. Somewhere, spread in the field, were the ashes of hundreds of fires. Maybe sucked up by a root, added to a vegetable, cooked again.

They stood just outside the bedroom door, telling each other "Good night," back and forth.

"Good night, Laurel."

"Good night, Will."

"Good night, Laurel."

I concentrated on the bowl of my pipe. I inhaled, and held in the smoke.

"You're still up?" she said, closing the door behind her.

She'd undone her braid. All these daily rituals I never saw. Her standing there, pulling her hair out of its braid, getting ready for bed. And then braiding it back up before starting the day. Her hair was longer than I expected, far past her shoulders. It made her look younger.

"Close your eyes," she said.

I did, and heard her change into her nightgown. She got under the covers, as far away from me as possible.

"Have you always done that?" she said. "Puffing away up there?"

"Some nights," I said.

"I'm surprised you didn't suffocate yourself."

I closed my eyes and let the back of my head rest on the wall. The sand in my hair crunched as I turned it from side to side, massaging my scalp on the knots in the wood.

"Who is he?" I said.

At first, she didn't say anything from under the covers.

"I knew him before I knew your father," she said.

"In Concord?" I said.

"Yes."

She didn't say any more, and I didn't know what else to ask.

"How long is he staying?" I said.

"I don't know," she said. "But some time. And I don't know what we're going to do about the girl."

I doused the tobacco with my thumb. Out the door, a still-warm fire. Around the house, sand dunes shifted one grain at a time.

✦

RAIN CRACKLING ON the roof woke me. Wide awake. Pure awake. The wind punched the windows. The bed shrieked when Laurel moved. Rain gurgled through the shingles. Waterfalls pounded the ground in a constant whine. A wet wind had found our roof and was gnawing at it.

I hadn't been sleeping much anyway. It started the summer before, when I'd wake in the night and stay up nearly until sunrise. I might make tea and walk down the beach. In the summer I weeded the gardens. On my hands and knees under the stars, picking grasses. It made me feel good, to wake in the morning to a pile of uprooted weeds by a patch of cucumbers, for instance. It was like I had gained a short, dark day nested in the night. I sometimes fell asleep in the garden, in the barn, or against the side of the house.

I left the bed. The fireplace still glowed from under the ash. From the cellar, cider barrels plugged with cloth bungs hissed. When winter came, I'd roll a keg outside to freeze out layers of ice, night by night, until all that was left was the alcohol that coldness couldn't pull any ice from.

I lit a rushlight and took Will's satchel from the peg by the door to my chair by the fire. The bottle with its trapped pear was still at the foot of Will's chair.

I laid out the contents: a shirt, string, a razor blade, paintbrushes. I piled them on the floor. Under that, small glass jars. One was a jar of sticky brown substance, almost like beeswax. Under the bottles was a notebook. Not the one he'd been using earlier that night. It had a soft leather cover with a worn, peeling spine. Overstuffed with papers. I lit another rushlight and opened it on my lap.

Stretching across two pages was a drawing of a breaking wave. Then, a juniper branch full of berries. A cloud passing over the landscape. A shadowy copse of trees. A woman floating in the water, her hair fanning from her head. And scattered throughout, pages of the same woman. Then one of a man hanging from the gallows. And finally, near the end, before the book's gasp of blank pages continuing to the back cover, a stack of loose papers. Letters.

They were in Laurel's handwriting. The first one I read was about wanting to see him again, that she missed him. The next one was blunter. The final letter confirmed what I knew in her sweat and her eyes. "I am unwell," she wrote. "Edwin is fine—so it's deep in me somewhere. You will not be sick if you come. When you come."

I held those two letters side by side. One dated a few weeks after the other. Like two sides of a scale. I am unwell. Come. Please, she'd ended one letter. Please. Comma. Laurel. As if she were pleading with herself. The date, on the upper corner, two months after Dad drowned.

We rarely sent out the post—mostly to my grandparents in Concord who came twice a year. When we did, we gave the letters to Paul, who would row his and our parcels to town. I wondered when she'd given the letters to him. Or if Paul had kept the responses hidden from me. She might have walked down Coatue, hailed a boat, and handed them off herself.

I stacked the letters neatly in the back of the notebook and retied the twine. I waited for the flame to finish its path down the rush while I listened to the rain. Our roof was a drumhead.

I replaced the notebook in the satchel. Footsteps scraped sand on the floorboards upstairs.

Ben Shattuck is a writer and painter from coastal Massachusetts. A graduate and former Teaching-Writing Fellow of the Iowa Writers' Workshop, he is now the director of the Cuttyhunk Island Writers' Residency and the curator of the Dedee Shattuck Gallery. His writing has appeared in the *Harvard Review*, *The New Republic*, *The Paris Review Daily*, *The Common*, *Salon.com*, *McSweeney's Internet Tendency*, and *Lit Hub*. His paintings have been exhibited in galleries, including the Steven Amedee Gallery in New York, the New Bedford Art Museum and Sloane Merrill Gallery in Boston, and the Greylock Gallery in Williamstown, Massachusetts. "Edwin Chase of Nantucket" is part of a novel he is currently writing.

EDITOR'S NOTE

Truths and fictions, the lies we spin and make ourselves believe, the unrest and confusion of a warring world in all its chaos: Ruth Serven ties all this together with an infectious energy in her story "A Message," published in our Fall 2016 issue. Serven has created a narrator who is at once agile, playful, conversational, and completely engaging. It's a story that manages—impressively, in fewer than 1,400 words—to involve us on a personal, political, and universal level.

This is a short and slippery story, and that is what we loved about it: the narrative voice, to say the least, is unexpected. It circles around the ongoing pursuit of an unknown and enigmatic father, whose identity and lack of contact are a mystery. The narrator's approach is the equivalent of drawing a piece of puzzle and seeing if it might fit.

Serven is a journalist who also writes fiction. In "A Message," there is a sense of the investigator who is open to every conclusion, always searching for an elusive truth. This is a story that doesn't depend on "tired tropes and plot holes," as Serven explained to us. Instead, she has come to think of it "as a continual 'coming-out process,' of revealing what is already in my own head or subconscious."

Odette Heideman, editor
Epiphany

A MESSAGE

Ruth Serven

PERHAPS IT BEGINS like this, you say earnestly to your disbelieving friend in a coffee shop, or the secondhand store, or the line to buy banitsa at the metro stop—

—perhaps, no listen to me, my father, Stefan, had to go back to Serbia for business. Perhaps his passport was stolen by a nationalist. He rushed to the embassy to get a new one. But the embassy was overwhelmed by refugees and worried about terrorists, though of course he wasn't one. Irena the receptionist told him to come back another day, but every day was the same. He had leva in his pocket that the bank did not want, and not enough euros to pay the right lawyers and border guards.

He stayed in Belgrade to work, and got an apartment. Every day he told himself, I must go back, I must return to my family, but he was never able to get away. He is very important. He works all weekends and holidays. But someday he will finally get away for Christmas or summer holiday and take me to the sea.

The train passes.

You say you do not have money for the metro anyway. We can just walk to the park. We circle the lily pond and talk about boys and music. You ask me to quiz you for your next English test. You sing the new Britney song. *All around the world, pretty girls.*

Perhaps it begins like this, you start again—

—it was during the new Republic. And we were getting things from France and the States finally, clothes and cars and toilet paper, but no one had any money and the government was collapsing. And my father came to Sofia to flee the wars in Serbia, which was then Yugoslavia.

One day he was walking in the Borisova Gradina, and he saw a woman playing a violin on the steps by the lily pond. He stopped to tell her how beautiful her playing was, and they began talking, and then he asked if he could take her out to dinner. They talked and talked all evening and then they went back to her apartment.

They were going to get married, but my father had to return to Serbia to take care of some property matters. They could not afford to talk on the phone and this was before the internet. He was going to return immediately, but you know how the Serbians are, everything takes forever, and I was born before he could return.

You haven't met my mother, but let me tell you: She is crazy. When things were settled, my father asked if he could return and marry her but she said no, she had had the baby by herself, and she was going to raise me by herself. And then she moved and he could not find her again. But she still gave me his last name, which is Blankov, which is how I was able to find him. She also gave me this stupid first name, which you must never call me.

The train passes.

Perhaps it begins like this—

—I knew his last name. I told my neighbor about my mother and my father, and Vesi said she would help me find him. She is a very nice person; we cook meals together and share flour and milk. We searched and searched, but there are too many Blankovs in Belgrade. It took a very long time. Sometimes Vesi despaired but I always cheered her up, and we kept looking. Finally we found him, first name Stefan. He had been an adviser for the government! I found a picture of him standing with our king, would you believe it? They're shaking hands in front of the old palace in Sofia. I printed off the picture. I keep it in my purse, here. So if I see him, I'll recognize him.

The train passes.

You say you have fought with Vesi and are not speaking to her. You fight with everyone, have fought with Vesi before, but usually you make up quickly. This time, you will not say why you fought. You say it makes you too angry to talk about.

You say your mother has left again. She works in France as a caretaker for an old man. The jobs are bad in Bulgaria and many people leave for other countries in Europe. Your mother sends money back, but it barely covers the rent and you are left to scrounge leva for food and clothes and phone minutes. You are very thin. You invite yourself over for dinner, and I make tacos, but you say they are too spicy.

We often go to the mall. Usually to H&M. Your mother is planning to pay for a new computer before you begin university, but you wonder if she might turn the money into a clothing allowance.

Perhaps you can get a job and pay for clothes that way. We go look in the windows of each store that is hiring. But at every place, you say you couldn't possibly work there—it is too ugly, too dirty, too small. Everything in Bulgaria is like this, you say.

We walk back down the street. We part ways and you get on a bus.

I know he has other children, you say once. We are in a bookshop, flipping idly through journals. What?

You say you've met a half brother. You found him through Facebook and went to his apartment in Iztok. You didn't tell him who you were. You said you were selling subscriptions and he said he didn't want any. Then he shut the door. That was it, the end. He was tall, like you, but of course you're more attractive. You thought about knocking again but you were afraid.

You say you know there are others. You say your father loved a lot of women.

You say that someday you'll find each of your siblings. Your father will buy a house and you'll all live together. Like *Full House*.

The train passes.

Perhaps it begins like this—

—one bottle too many of Zgorka, a dark room, an expired condom. Do things like this still happen? A note in the morning swept up by wind from the mountain. Twenty years of lost messages, until one photo, one name, one message breaks through, just like I knew it would, and some day he'll get on a train—

The train passes.

Perhaps it begins like this—

—one bottle too many of Zgorka, a dark room, an expired condom, no note in the morning.

I asked you once if you wanted me to contact Stefan for you. I asked if you wanted to send a letter to his address in Belgrade. How would I know what to write? you asked, twisting your hands. I asked if I should write the letter. No, never, you said, you would refuse to speak to me.

Still, I looked up the word for *stamps* in my dictionary, and I walked to the post office and jigsawed five different kinds of international stamps onto the envelope. Meet me at the station in Sofia in five days, I wrote, and I can take you to your daughter.

I wait and wait at the train station. I see people pour out of the coach from Belgrade, from Bucharest, from Istanbul.

The trains come; the trains pass.

Perhaps the train was late, perhaps the luggage was lost, perhaps wind from the mountain blew my note away. Perhaps there are a million reasons. I write all this in a note so that there is one more way for Stefan to find us, so that there is one more way for him to come home. I put the note on the bench.

A train passes.

Then I write another note to you, Lana, so you know that someone remembers all the stories, all the ways you thought Stefan might have left you, all the times you wished he would come back. I write so you know someone listened. Maybe we will not speak again, maybe we cannot be friends again, maybe this note will be

thrown away after you pick up your poshta, but, still—here is this
message.

I stand up as another train is coming in.

———————

Ruth Serven is a creative writer and journalist in the flyover states. She is a native of Oklahoma City and a proud graduate of the Missouri School of Journalism.

EDITOR'S NOTE

Amber Caron's "The Handler" stood out to our editors for many reasons, among them its bounty of wonderful sensory details, its assuredness of voice, its deft pacing, and the power with which it expresses human resiliency. The surging sense of well-being that a person feels in achieving freedom from need animates the story's climax. The breakthrough does not arrive in a drumroll epiphany but sneaks up quietly as it does in life, amid simple, quotidian routine. When this moment of grace appears, the trembling leaves of the aspen trees sound like "polite applause," but the protagonist—politeness be damned—feels the sudden urge to howl for joy.

Greg Brownderville, editor in chief
Southwest Review

THE HANDLER

Amber Caron

THE MORNING LESLIE arrived in Jefferson, New Hampshire, Brent picked her up from the bus station wearing ripped jeans and a flannel shirt that had been cut at the elbows. It was twenty-five degrees. It was January. It appeared he was sweating. He opened the passenger-side door, put his hand on her back, and helped her into the truck. Leslie guessed he was older than she was but younger than her father. She found it difficult to name a man's age.

"Moved here in '95," he said. "Never got around to leaving." He sped up around the hairpin turns, pointing out every bend in the river, every mountain peak, every place there had ever been a car accident serious enough to kill. Each crash site was marked with a yellow ribbon and a bundle of fake sunflowers. She suspected he was responsible for them. The flowers, not the accidents. He steered with his knees so he could light his cigarette, and Leslie forced herself not to grab the door handle.

He kept talking. Constellations. Moon cycles. The flood of '97. The blizzard of '99. The fire of '05. When they finally pulled up to the house, the dogs erupted, and Brent went quiet.

✦

SIBERIANS, ALASKAN MALAMUTES, Akitas, Russian wolf-
hounds, salukis, Saint Bernards, and mongrels—greyhounds mixed
with Newfoundlands and a dash of Belgian shepherd; Labradors
mixed with coonhounds. Their names had been painted on the
green wooden boxes they slept in: Mars, Frost, McGee, Bandit,
Minnow, Tip, Empire, Stewpot, Pluto. Back of the property was the
Scooby-Doo litter: Velma, Scooby, Shaggy, Daphne. Next to them,
the pianists: Billy Joel, Elton John.

"That there is Ray Charles," Brent said, pointing to the glassy-
eyed dog at the end of the line. "Was named Ray Charles before he
went blind."

Leslie bent over to take the dog's muzzle in her hands. His nose
twitched. He lifted a paw.

"Well, maybe you should start naming them after billionaires,"
Leslie said.

"I like it. A sense of humor. That will help you here." He bent
down, held Billy Joel's nose to his. "What's that, Billy? How'd this
lady get here? Well, you'll just have to ask her."

Brent stared up at Leslie. "Well, answer the dog," he whispered.
"Ruff."

"Billy Joel, are you going to accept that answer?"

The dog rolled over onto his back.

The truth was that the night before she boarded the bus for New
Hampshire, she left her boyfriend, Dennis, a voicemail: *I'm leaving you. This time for the woods and fifty-seven dogs.* It sounded
funnier when she'd rehearsed it in her head. She waited all night for
him to call back and talk her out of it.

"First and foremost, your job is to take care of their paws." Brent
brought the dog's front paw close to his face. "No paw, no dog."

He said it again, like a mantra, and taught Leslie how to check for ice balls between their toes; lacerations, abrasions, swelling, and cracks on the pads; abscesses and inflamed nail beds. "These paws need to get me from Anchorage to Nome in three months."

Fifty-seven dogs. Two hundred and twenty-eight paws. She wanted to show it all to Dennis.

THE FIRST NIGHT she couldn't sleep through the country sounds. Wind in the trees. Dogs calling to a distant coyote howl. A train on the other side of the valley. When the sun came up, Leslie's eyes had already adjusted to the light.

She dressed and went outside. Brent was waiting on the front stoop of her cabin, halfway through a sentence she had to imagine the beginning of:

". . . dry food. A hunk of frozen beef. A ladle of chicken broth. Twice a day. While they eat, you scoop their shit into this bucket, and dump it over there past that stand of pines." Brent pointed in a vague direction. There were pine trees everywhere. She followed him to the shed behind her cabin.

"And you'll want this, too." Brent pulled an ice pick from a hook. "The shit freezes over night. Got to chip it into the bucket."

It took Leslie three and a half hours to finish morning chores. By the time she had rounded up the empty bowls, cleaned the yard, and checked all two hundred and twenty-eight paws, she had three blisters on her palm and a bloody shin where she'd clipped herself with the ice pick. One of the dogs had lunged for her ear, three dogs tried to hump her leg, and another mounted her back. At 10 a.m., her stomach was still empty, but the smell of blood from the raw beef made her want to retch. She forced herself to drink some water, which sloshed around in her stomach. *Not funny anymore*, she thought.

Brent stepped out onto the porch of the big house across the valley where he waved Leslie over. She trudged across the snowy lawn and found him standing at the stove in the kitchen, a book in his hands, a line of jars on the counter. He pulled out a large pot from beneath the sink.

"We make our own salve," he said. "Too expensive to buy the other stuff. And it's got a bunch of crap in it, anyway. This is all you need."

She looked at the ingredients: Vaseline, Betadine, lanolin, glycerine, vitamin A, vitamin E.

He pointed at the stove. "I'll help you with this first batch."

Leslie measured and poured according to the recipe. Brent talked and stirred and talked more. Behind her, Leslie heard footsteps coming down the hall. A girl appeared in her pajamas, her hair in a high ponytail, eyes wide like Brent's.

"My daughter, Jill," Brent said. He handed Leslie the wooden spoon and put his arm around the girl as though they were posing for a picture. She shrugged him off. "This is Leslie," he said, pointing toward the stove. Jill rolled her eyes and reached for the bananas on the counter. Leslie turned back to the salve and pretended not to be offended, and the girl dragged her feet down the hall and slammed a door.

"Some advice: Don't have kids until scientists figure out a way to skip age thirteen."

Leslie did the math. Her own child would have been one. Tantrums. Diapers. Meltdowns.

"She's not a talker," Brent said.

"I wasn't at thirteen either."

"I mean she's deaf. She signs, reads lips."

"So I shouldn't take that whole scene personally?"

"No, you should," he said. "She wants to go to Alaska with me in March to help with the dogs. When our handler quit last month she thought she was a sure thing since no one before you has ever taken this job in the middle of the winter."

Leslie had never been to Alaska, had never even considered it before.

"Shouldn't she be in school?"

"Maybe." Brent moved the pot off the burner and grabbed a funnel from under the sink and a line of tiny vials. "She hates it. I don't push the issue."

"But there are laws." She filled a vial, held it up to the light.

"You think anyone's coming out here to see what a deaf girl and her musher dad are up to?"

"She needs an education. I mean, even a high school education."

"You go to school?" he asked.

"Yeah. College. A few years of grad school."

"And here we both are."

AT THE END of the first week, Leslie wrote Dennis a letter. She told him how the dogs ran for hours on the trails beyond the pines, and still they barked, cried, howled for more. She told him how she clipped nails, wrapped paws in booties, and massaged pads with the salve. She kept a small vial of the medicine tucked close to her body so it would stay warm. This made it easier to massage into the paws, and the vials made her feel like a doctor. At the end of the letter she wrote, *Come for a visit. I'll teach you.*

When a week passed without hearing from him, she wrote another letter. Each day she checked the mailbox at the end of the long dirt driveway.

✦

ALL SHE HAD eaten in her first two weeks was canned soup and granola bars, so when Brent invited her to the big house for pork chops and mashed potatoes, she accepted.

Before they had even finished loading their plates, Brent started talking. Race strategy, dog diets, harnesses. He'd raced the Iditarod twice, the Yukon Quest three times. He spoke slowly, story after story of his victories, of his run-ins with moose, of the time he rounded a corner on day thirteen of his first Iditarod and found an old boat frozen in the middle of the Yukon River. It was a sign, he said. He knew he'd win.

"But really it was bootying the dogs that won it. Bootied every one in under twenty seconds at every stop. Shaved three hours off my time. That was the difference between first place and third last year in the Quest," he said.

Jill didn't take her eyes off her father's lips. Leslie watched them, too. They were chapped, a firm line down the middle like a cut that might open any time. More gray than pink. When he chewed, the tiny hairs of his moustache and beard touched.

"In her first race," he nodded at Jill, "she was disqualified when she took a wrong turn two miles in and raced the entire course backwards."

Jill sat up straight now, leaned in closer when Brent tipped his head toward his plate.

"People tried to stop her, but she thought they were just cheering her on. She finished last. Two hours after everyone else. An hour after dark."

Jill swiped her hands through the air; Brent watched them. He laughed.

"She says blame Sass, her lead dog." He looked back at his daughter. "User error, I'd say."

Jill's hands danced.

"My fault?" Brent said.

She went on. When Jill finally rested her fingers on the table, Leslie noticed calluses and cuts, dirt lodged beneath her nails. Brent kept chewing. Jill pointed at him, then at Leslie. She did it again, this time nodding her head, opening her eyes wide.

Finally, he swallowed: "Says it's my fault for not letting her take my team."

Jill looked at Leslie, nodded her head once. Leslie tried to smile at her. Jill was unmoved. *We will not be friends*, that look said. She sliced her hands through the air again and this time Brent put his fork down. When she finished, they stared at each other for a long time.

"I'm not telling her that," Brent said.

Jill stood up from the table, flipped her father off, walked through the dark house, and slammed a door.

ANOTHER WEEK PASSED. More letters. She told Dennis that even when temperatures dropped below zero the dogs had only hay to keep them warm. They slept with their tails over their noses. When they woke, they ran laps around their houses for something to do, perfect little racetracks of packed snow. The swivel at the end of each of their chains clinked against the post, and the yard sounded like a chorus of finger tambourines. *Come for a visit. Soon. Before I leave for Alaska.*

She was making her morning rounds when Brent returned from the mailbox with an envelope. The handwriting she would have known even without the name in the corner, and she took it inside where she held it to the light and peered at the small piece of paper inside. No bigger than a Post-it note. She ripped a neat strip from the edge of the envelope, turned it upside down, dumped the note onto her tiny wooden table. It was written on the paper Dennis kept on the edge of his desk—the one with a picture of a pipe in the bottom right hand corner. He hated the paper, but his mother had bought it for him when he turned thirty and gave up chewing to-bacco for a pipe; and although Leslie had tried to get him to throw it away a dozen times, he said he felt too guilty. Instead, he used it for trivial matters. Grocery lists. To-do lists. Killing spiders.

She unfolded the paper. *Stop. Stop writing to—*

Leslie didn't read the rest. She tucked the note back inside the envelope, found a clean sheet of paper, and sat down with a pen.

Dennis,

Stewpot has a fissure; Mars, a swollen ankle. Scooby's dewclaw is inflamed because I put his bootie on wrong. It started just as an irritation, but I ignored it, and now Scooby might be done for the season. Come visit next Saturday. It's lonely here.

Love,
Leslie

THEY HAD BEEN here before, the two of them. The first time she broke up with him—the first warm day of spring two years ago, she remembered, the ground soaked with melted snow—he delivered a pile of soil to her backyard because she once said she wanted a garden. Each day after that, he left her packages of tiny seeds—corn, squash, carrots, chard, broccoli, cauliflower, banana peppers, red peppers, bell peppers—until finally, weeks later, on the day he brought her pumpkin seeds, she called him and said *Fine, okay, stop with the seeds.* Six months later, when he ended it, it was her turn to lure him back, and she did it with ripe tomatoes, crookneck squash, overflowing bags of green beans, and bundles of basil. When he wouldn't open his door, she left the vegetables on his doorstep, adding to the rotting pile on her way to the bank, until one morning she showed up, doorstep clear of the rot, to find a note: *Come in*, it said.

She got laid off from her job a week later and was pregnant just a month after that. He thought maybe they could do it. Maybe that child—and marriage, he said—was exactly what they needed. But the money, she'd insisted. He was only part-time at the warehouse. And besides, she'd already made the appointment. He said nothing more and showed up at the clinic where they held hands the way they had when they started dating. Leslie tried to ignore how sad he was in the weeks after, and she tried to hide her immediate relief, but once a week they yelled about it until she boarded the bus for New Hampshire. She hadn't expected to miss him.

With this new letter in hand, she walked to the end of the driveway, the dogs calling after her, and shoved it into the mailbox.

SHE WAS SCRUBBING the harnesses in the warming shed. Brent came in to stack the large green bags of food. The water in the bucket had cooled, and Leslie had to steel herself before she plunged each harness. The blisters on her hand were threatening to burst.

Later she would poke each one with a needle and watch the skin sink back into itself.

"I was wondering if I could have Saturday off," Leslie said. She moved the harness from the wash bucket to the rinse bucket, where the water was slightly warmer.

Brent hauled two loads of food from the wheelbarrow to the corner twice before he spoke. "Going somewhere?"

"Someone's coming to visit," she said. "Just for the day. My fiancé." The word had slipped out, but Leslie found comfort in it. It was familiar and full of hope. She let it hang there. It had been true, almost.

Brent removed the ladder from the hooks at the far end of the shed and set it up in front of the stack he'd made. He climbed, holding on with one hand, balancing a bag on his shoulder with the other. He reached the top, flung the bag onto the stack, and waited there for a moment to catch his breath. Leslie saw him look at her left hand. She pushed it deep into the water.

"Do your morning chores. Then you can have the rest of the day." He didn't look at her when he said it.

On Friday morning while Jill watched her do the chores, Leslie couldn't help but feel the girl was collecting evidence of her insufficiency. After all the shit had been collected and the dogs each fed, Jill went from doghouse to doghouse, peering into the doors, talking to the dogs with her hands. She coaxed Sass out with treats and inspected her paws, pulled the skin back at the dog's cheek and scraped at her teeth. She rubbed the dog's chest, ran her hands down each leg, scanned the underside of the tail and inside the ears. Satisfied that Leslie hadn't ruined her lead dog, Jill tipped her head back and made her mouth into a tight circle, blowing puffs of hot air. Sass did the same, howling along to Jill's silent call.

THAT AFTERNOON, JILL walked the perimeter of the property with a small white book. She stopped in front of a trunk, placed her hand against the bark, flipped pages, looked up, walked around the tree, flipped more pages. On and on, all afternoon. When Jill waved Leslie over, Leslie didn't move, certain Jill's gesture had not been for her. Jill waved again, this time with more urgency. Leslie went.

She wasn't sure what to do around the girl, where to put her hands, how to stop her vocal instinct.

Jill pointed to the tree. The bark was white and scarred with black lines, as if it had been lashed with a burning whip. She turned to the section near the end of her tree guide. She put her finger on the bottom of the page. *Quaking aspen.* Scientific name: *Tremuloides.* Jill put her hand into her coat and pulled out a pen and a small notebook, flipped until she found a blank page, scribbled something, and handed the notebook to Leslie, covering her mouth with her hand.

Like hemorrhoids.

Leslie rolled her eyes, but her smile betrayed her.

Jill pointed to the woods and then back at the book. She swept her arms through the air and pointed again.

Leslie shook her head, shrugged her shoulders. Jill tried again, pointing from the book to the woods and to the book again. She stared hard at Leslie, waiting.

"Okay," Leslie said. "Show me."

Jill smiled, tucked her book in her coat. They walked together across the field, beyond the doghouses and the food shed. The morning wind had settled, but clouds were coming in from the south. Two crows were fighting in the pines. Somewhere a woodpecker was pounding on a tree trunk. Just before they entered the woods, Leslie heard a door slam, its echo holding for a moment in the valley before lifting into the gray sky. She turned. Jill followed Leslie's eyes. They watched Brent get into the truck holding an armful of yellow ribbons and fake sunflowers and disappear down the driveway.

Jill was scribbling something in her notebook. She handed it to Leslie. *Let's run his team. Out to the aspen.*

Leslie shook her head. She pointed toward the driveway.

Jill wrote again: *Changes all the ribbons at the crash sites! Gone all day.*

When Leslie pointed to the dogs, Jill wrote, *I'll help.*

When Leslie pointed to the sky, Jill wrote, *Tonight. No weather till tonight!*

Finally, Leslie took the pad and pen and wrote her own message: *I'll get fired.*

Jill took the pen from her hand, scribbled something and handed it back. *He likes you.* Jill took it again and drew three heavy lines beneath the word *likes* and pushed it back into Leslie's hands. Then Jill gave her a look like she was stupid. She pointed to the word she'd underlined and opened her eyes wide.

Swift, methodical, careful, Jill harnessed four dogs in the time it took Leslie to hitch one. With the towline anchored to the barn, all nine dogs lunged forward and leapt off the ground. Jill climbed onto the runners and Leslie sat in the cargo bag, tucked between the dog treats, snow hook, and blankets. When Jill released the towline from the barn wall, the dogs sprinted forward, leaving the forty-eight others howling behind.

They headed west past her cabin and the warming shed, out beyond the aspen they had studied together, hugging the base of the mountains. The dogs kicked up snow as they ran, and Leslie shielded her eyes as best she could. But she wanted to watch them, the way the wheel dogs lunged forward and the swing dogs guided the team around the corners. They'd given up their howls for heavy panting, the occasional grunt. They worked. They did their job.

Once through the valley, they entered a stand of maples, oaks, and spruce. The bare limbs towered above them and the forest became a shadow of itself, dark despite the daylight, and the entire world—the snow, the trees, the bits of sky above, even the backs of the dogs—blurred together into a mass of gray. Jill guided the dogs and the sled through the trees, along a trail that had been traveled before but covered by recent snow. It wasn't until they were deep into the woods that Leslie saw the forest open up on hundreds of thin white aspen.

Leslie felt the sled slow, and just before they came to a stop, Jill dropped the snow hook, the two steel prongs sinking deep into the ground. Stewpot and Mars, the workhorses in the wheel, looked back. Bandit plopped down in the fresh snow. Minnow peed.

Jill pulled her book out of her jacket and waved for Leslie to follow her. Beneath the trees, Jill opened the book and pushed it into Leslie's hand. She learned that a stand of aspen grew up to twenty acres of roots before sprouting an entire family of trunks, that every tree in a clone of aspen was genetically identical. She learned that birch bark peeled and blistered in the sun, but that aspen never lost its skin.

Leslie heard the dogs behind them getting restless. A sneeze, a whimper, Bandit and Mars pawing each other in play. But Inca's head was lowered, and the fur on her back raised. Leslie followed the dog's gaze.

Beyond the aspen, a patch of brown. Too big to be a coyote, too dark to be a deer. Whatever it was disappeared behind the spruce trees, and rather than seeing the thing—bear? human?—Leslie could only trace the movement of the figure by the changing light through the trees.

The rest of the dogs, as though on Inca's cue, directed their attention to whatever was out there. Jill, still standing out by the aspen, hadn't noticed. Leslie watched until the figure emerged from behind the tall brush and into the edge of the opening.

Leslie tapped Jill on the shoulder, pointed. Jill dropped her book and ran for the team. The moose stared at the group for a long time, and the dogs pulled hard against their line. The snow hook didn't budge. When the dogs broke out in growls and barks, the moose took two steps forward. Jill swung her arms at the dogs in a silent command: Stay. The moose moved forward again, hooves disappearing into the fresh snow with each step. On the back of the sled, Jill pulled hard at the brake. All nine dogs lunged. The snow hook came loose. The dogs gave chase. The moose charged.

Jill tried to slow the team by tipping the sled. Leslie ran to help her, but it was already too late. The moose stomped its way through the dogs, tangling its legs in the gangline. A sharp, collective yelp went up from the pack. The moose rose up and took aim at the sled. Its front legs crashed down on the runners and Jill and Leslie fell to the ground. Leslie screamed at the dogs to stop, but nothing she said worked. Jill reached for the snow hook. When the moose stood up on its back legs again, an entire team of dogs biting at its backside, Jill swung the snow hook wildly, catching the loose skin under the animal's chin. The moose threw back its antlers, let out a guttural growl, and ran. It dragged the dogs and the sled behind it, until finally the towline caught on the trunk of an aspen, and the prongs ripped clean from the moose's chin. The animal slipped deeper into the woods, leaving a heavy trail of blood.

Leslie scanned her own body. She expected to be injured, but she wasn't. She hurried over to Jill, who pushed herself up onto her elbow and held her side. Leslie gently pushed her down so she lay flat on her back and ran for blankets in the sled. When Leslie returned, Jill pointed at the dogs.

Bandit—poor Bandit—gave Leslie a pitiful look as she un-wrapped the tugline that had knotted around his neck. Minnow held up her back left paw, and when Leslie looked at it, she saw a slice down the center pad. She found a bootie in the sled pocket, wiped the snow from between the dog's pads, and secured the strap around the leg.

She untangled the rest of the dogs, checked their paws and ears and ribs and legs. At the center of the pile of animals was Inca, still on the ground. Leslie knelt next to her, put her hand to the dog's chest—warm, but barely moving. She put her ear up to the dog's face and heard a long, low rattling. At the end of each breath, a groan.

By the time Leslie lifted Inca and Jill onto the front of the sled and got the pack reharnessed, the line of moose blood had frozen and turned black. Slowly, the team pulled their group back the way they came—through the aspen grove, back along the base of the mountain—and Leslie watched Jill stroke Inca's ears.

BRENT PROPPED JILL up on her bed, pressed his hands to her shoulder blades, her stomach, her ribs.

"Three ribs, at least," Brent said. He didn't suggest a hospital and when Jill twisted her fingers through the air and dropped her eyes, Brent watched but went outside without responding.

Jill reached for the pen and paper next to her bed. *He won't speak to me.*

Leslie took the notebook. *It wasn't your fault.*

User error, Jill wrote.

I should have said no. I shouldn't have helped you. I wanted him to fire you. I wanted to go.

Leslie took the notebook. *You're thirteen.*

He'll take you to Alaska instead.

I don't want to go.

This was a lie. All she wanted was to go anywhere except across the field to the cabin she knew was dark and cold, where she would fall asleep alone on a cot in a sleeping bag that kept her alive but never warm.

Jill took the notebook. *What did it sound like?*

The moose?

No. Inca, dying.

Nothing, Leslie wrote. *She died immediately.*

Will you talk to him for me?

He'll get over it. They're just dogs.

You don't know him very well.

Jill pointed to her pillow, and when Leslie tried to fix it for her, Jill shook her head vigorously back and forth. Leslie tried to shift it again, but Jill squinted her eyes, pushed herself up on her elbow, and fixed the pillow herself.

Leslie left her there and went out to check on Minnow. She pulled the vial from the breast pocket of her jacket, poured the salve into the palm of her hand, and massaged the dog's paw. Minnow she could touch without hurting.

✦

Brent was in the warming shed when Leslie went in to make dinner for the dogs. It wasn't until she'd filled the water bucket in the sink that she saw Inca stretched across the ground, her legs straight and stiffened, perfectly still, her head propped on a blanket, as though she were asleep.

"She's sorry," Leslie said. "So am I."

"We'll have to get Sass ready. She'll take Inca's place." He rubbed the fur on Inca's neck.

"You have to talk to her. She feels terrible."

He ran his hands down Inca's legs, cupped her front paws, and tucked them into the black trash bag he'd placed at her feet. "We've got a month, which, for a dog like Sass, is plenty of time. She'll do fine." He tucked Inca's back legs into the bag, then her tail.

"I can get her harnessed up tomorrow," Leslie said.

"No," he said. "Do the morning chores. Then take the afternoon off like I promised." He pushed the bag up under her stiffened legs until he got it up to her neck. He ran his hand over Inca's face, gave each ear a scratch. "For your boyfriend."

"I'll help you bury her."

"Ground is frozen."

"What then?"

"The dump. They'll let me put her in the incinerator."

He pulled the bag over the dog's face, tied a knot, and hefted it into his arms. He walked to the door, the veins on his arms bulging beneath the black bag.

"Fiancé," she said.

Brent turned around. "What?"

"Not my boyfriend. My fiancé."

"Right."

Leslie watched him walk toward the truck and could see his lips moving. She knew he was whispering to Inca. The yard was silent, the rest of the dogs tucked in their houses, a few snouts resting at the opening of their green boxes, sniffing at the air behind the dead dog.

THAT NIGHT, WEATHER came in. Snow, wind, ice, more snow. The line of spruce trees, their tops hunched over, looked as if they were running from the wind. The oaks groaned; two aspen snapped. The birds clutched branches and then disappeared on some invisible current. Even in the cabin, the wind pulled the heat from Leslie's neck, her cheeks, her eyes. Then it became all she could hear.

On Saturday, Leslie woke thinking of how, on the morning after they visited the clinic, Dennis had rolled over in bed, grabbed her hand, put it on his chest, and said it hurt *right there*. She'd pulled her hand away and left him in bed alone. But she felt it now, that darkness in her chest, and all she could think to do was climb out of her cot, layer herself against the cold, and do the morning chores. Food, shit, hay, paws.

Outside, the entire world glimmered white in the bright sun, but the snow, all eleven inches of it with a thin layer of ice on top, looked razor-edged and dangerous. She heard Brent in the barn, and when she went in, he was already working on Sass. He pushed an electric razor in and out of the pads of her paws, spread her toes, and trimmed around each nail. It was supposed to be Leslie's job. He lit a long taper candle and, moving the flame across the shaved pad, singed the hairs that were too small and too deep for the razor to reach. When the hairs sparked, Leslie expected Sass to yelp the way the dogs always did for her, but the dog, staring straight ahead at the barn wall, didn't move, didn't make a sound. Before long

the barn was filled with the awful stink of charred hair, and Leslie
went back to her cabin.

Inside, she showered, put on her cleanest jeans and a real bra,
not the sports bra she'd been wearing since she arrived, and dried
her hair with the hair dryer she hadn't yet used. She left her hair
down because Dennis liked it best that way, and she skipped the lip
gloss because he didn't like the way it felt when they kissed.

She sat in the rocking chair next to the window and watched
Brent bootie up Sass. He straddled the dog, pushed the button
of his watch, and began: he lifted one of the back paws, pushed
the snow out of the pad, pulled the bootie on, wrapped the strap
around the leg. Three more paws. Twenty-seven seconds. He did it
again. Paw, push, pull, wrap. Twenty-five seconds. Again. Twenty-
three. Twenty. He stopped when he hit nineteen—as Leslie knew he
would—brought the dog back to her house, and walked across the
yard to his own.

For the rest of the day, Leslie tried not to think of Jill inside,
wrapped up in bed, holding her ribs. Or of Inca, her cold body in a
black bag, or Brent, lifting the dog into a fire. Instead, she sat down
to write another letter. She didn't tell Dennis to come for a visit because sometimes changing the subject worked better than begging.
She told him only that Inca had died, knowing he would find that
hard to ignore.

HOURS LATER, IN the dark, just before Leslie was about to give
up and crawl into her sleeping bag, the dogs stirred. Like toddlers,
Leslie thought. Screaming for attention, leaping onto their houses,
trying to out-howl the others. Every sound—squirrel, rabbit,
door—set them off.

Tonight she couldn't take it. She stood and reached for the door, but she heard someone climbing the steps to her cabin. It wasn't Brent—she knew his heavy gait. No, this was softer, less sure. A knock.

Leslie opened the door to find Jill hunched over a walking stick, furious and in tears.

She pushed a piece of paper at Leslie. *He hired our last handler to go with him.*

Jill snatched the paper back.

They're leaving next week! Three weeks early!

When Leslie didn't respond, Jill wrote more. *He's taking Sass. She's mine!*

You need rest.

I'm not going back in there.

Leslie led Jill to her cot and covered her with the sleeping bag. Once settled, Jill wrote again. *You have to stay.*

Leslie turned the light off next to the bed. The bare bulb in the kitchen was barely strong enough to light the room.

Jill held out the paper once more. *You look pretty.*

AFTER BRENT LEFT, Jill told Leslie that the two of them would race together the following season. Since she was still too frail to train the dogs, Jill trained Leslie instead. In the first week, she filled tiny notebooks of instructions that Leslie studied each night: Don't let them dip snow; don't let them play on the trail; be consistent; run McGee next to Legs, Basil next to Tarragon; give Pluto a good whack when he chases a rabbit; put Shaggy in the wheel, Velma in the lead. Make them work, that's what they want. In the second week, when Leslie confused the dogs with her commands, Jill pulled out a permanent marker and wrote *haw* on the top of Leslie's left mitten, *gee* on the top of her right. By the third week, Leslie was finally ready to run the full team.

Initially it was just in the morning, and she was always careful to stay within sight of the house. But then it was after lunch, too, and then, if the dogs seemed as though they wanted more—they always wanted more—she'd take them out on Saturday mornings along the base of the mountains. By the fourth week, she was running them for hours, sometimes without even realizing it, never telling Jill when she was leaving or when she'd be back. It wasn't just the warming air that she liked, and how it felt on her face. It was the buds popping out on the trees. And the dogs, too. The way they listened to her. The way they turned left when she yelled *haw*, the way they sprinted when she chanted *bring it on home*.

It was after one of these long morning runs that she returned to find Jill hanging a large map of Alaska on a bare kitchen wall.

Where were you? It was already written on the notepad.

Leslie pointed out past the warming shed, past her cabin.

For three hours!?

Leslie dug into her bag. She threw the dog treats on the floor, the headlamp, extra booties, the map, and the first aid kit, until she finally pulled out a book. It was wet from months of snow, and the pages curled up at the edges. The cover had faded, and the text was too blurry to read. But the tree on the front was still visible. Leslie had been looking for it on each of her runs that week.

Jill smiled, drew her fingers to her lips then stretched them forward, opening her callused palm.

"You're welcome," Leslie said.

They studied the map of Alaska, following Brent's journey, marking each stop with a tiny black dot. Anchorage to Campbell Airstrip to Willow and Yentna and Skwentna and Finger Lake, all twenty-three stops along the way to Nome. It wasn't until after she recorded the mileage between each checkpoint that Leslie thought of Dennis for the first time that day. She indulged in the memory of his persistence—the soil and the seeds, the impulsive proposal. She thought of how she once won him back with a pile of rotting vegetables, but how she'd failed with a letter about a dead dog. And as she watched Jill draw a large red circle around the notorious Dalzell Gorge and the equally treacherous Farewell Burn, Leslie noted she never once mentioned Jill in those letters. She was pleased with this fact, and she realized then she didn't want to show any of this to Dennis.

AFTER LUNCH, JILL went outside and practiced bootying Velma, and Leslie pulled a piece of paper from the stack by the phone and sat down to write a letter.

Brent,

I hung a yellow ribbon on the tree today, out where Inca died.

I couldn't find the sunflowers.

Leslie

She addressed it to the final checkpoint in Nome and walked to the mailbox.

✦

ON THE DAY Brent was set to cross the finish line, Leslie woke to a barking dog. Shaggy, she thought, more hound than husky. Another joined. Minnow, with that sharp little yelp. And another. Ray Charles, out there crying at all he couldn't see. She followed their calls into the yard and made her rounds. Carrying the bucket to the edge of the property, the aspen trees branched out above her, their trembling leaves like polite applause. As she returned to the yard, the dogs all mounted their houses, lifted their snouts to the open sky, and filled the air with long, dissonant howls. It was as close to a thank-you as Leslie ever got, and she had the irresistible urge to howl back.

———————

Amber Caron's work has appeared or is forthcoming in *Southwest Review*, *Kenyon Review Online*, *The Greensboro Review*, and *Agni*. She has an MFA from the Bennington Writing Seminars, where she was awarded the 2016 fiction prize. She is the recipient of the McGinnis-Ritchie Award for fiction from the *Southwest Review* and a grant from the Elizabeth George Foundation.

EDITOR'S NOTE

From the very first letter—a drop-cap *A* drawn in American Sign Language—"The Manual Alphabet" gets to work. This beautiful, tender, inventive meditation on language follows the story of a hearing boy born to deaf parents. As the parents teach the boy to speak with his hands, he begins to see the world in visual syntax, such as witnessing the birth of his sister: ". . . her arms and legs spelling endlessly. She looked like every letter at once." But as the boy advances in age, existential questions of identity emerge: Is he deaf or hearing? Is he the parent or child? It's not just that he's bilingual; it's that the two languages he speaks are based on entirely different senses, sight and sound, which gives him a unique perspective but also sharpens his isolation. He is both and he is neither. Written in short elegant fragments that are emphasized by the surrounding blankness of the page, the form adds to a growing feeling of isolation and probes the nature of memory. The writing itself is spectacular in its clarity.

When I discovered this piece, hiding among hundreds of anonymous submissions, it was that rarest of experiences, finding not a needle in a haystack, but a prince.

Trey Sager, fiction editor
Fence

THE MANUAL ALPHABET

Samuel Clare Knights

red face heaving fragile rib cage registering through my father's work shirt. My mother's pointed spectacles framing the mouth of a baby. "Is he deaf?" asked the nurses. Eyes reflected in a dry spoon on the Formica, my fair skin held upside down. "Who will hear him when he cries?"

And so Saginaw's fields went untouched and the plain would plain further. I learned to speak from a map and a kind neighbor. My mother shapes my hand with her hand. To be the boy is to be the map.

The map had silver lines embossed in the pulp that started to warp. I could see graphite fields and everything drawn there. Horizon began with a non-sense of floor and I was only as good as the color of each morning. This sheen was common, written over the same place and unknown to a commoner, as lavender as concrete with the composition of tinsel reserved for dusk. When the map moves, only things draped in its colors move with it. The metallic waves shimmer in the brown curl of the paper.

The place handed to me. By positioning fingers in certain ways, I thought I knew what they meant. Most of the time I would just point or make the shape. Created the sky by reaching out as far as I could on both sides and brought my hands low to cover it with clouds.

"Cow." C-O-W. Sign for cow: the thumb and pinky as horns twisting on a temple. Pull the airy udder for "milk." Each gesture possessed only the trace of a thing, in my mother's hands I saw quick palms that bent letters to their form; but especially the O, ringed and void, that made the fingers curve in around the microcosm of our living room—where mine would crystallize a little bleached moon, only more like a shadow puppet that still shows the arm of the object that casts it—her hands were the same ones that, before orbiting, patterned an entire world.

The ice storm in nineteen-seventy-something. How the power was out and the house was a dull song. I would sign to my mother through smoky breath. The letter *X* hooking our sleepy oxygen. The cold moved freely. My fingers trying to regard the filigree in the corner window. I couldn't say what I wanted.

I made an *S* and shook it in front of my face. My name dropped from a psalm. A same self flecked over an apparition. My letter started to blur as it shifted to the end: *palms*. Where the soft fist of Sam still hummed.

Comic books until 4 a.m., the Deaf smoking all night after a work-week with hearing people. I stayed up late and watched *Saturday Night Live*. On Monday none of the other kids knew the bits and the teachers looked concerned. I would go into a haze at school, missing my name several times before the silence caught me. My teachers thought I was going deaf when really I was somewhere else. Placing layers of gray on gray on gray. I would jolt back after going too far only to find Mrs. Groll's mouth moving. I knew it was time to grab my coat. Arrowwood Elementary had an outdoor white geodesic dome that I'd walk under to get to the principal's office. I was taken with the sounds bouncing off the inner circle. Something my parents would never know.

The teacher asked us to write about what we wanted to be. I wrote in place, one letter on top of the other until a graphite mass formed. A black key hung on a black wall. I smeared my fingers on it and signed letters to myself as fast as I could. The flight of my alphabet a bat vaporizing at my chest. My hand as good a voice as any.

The lake effect seemed normal. One day I missed the bus on purpose and walked across the field. A footfall cracking through ice, creating a long guide of where not to go. Before I broke the expanse I practiced on paper. Sitting in my room, making a slow tear through large sheets. I would listen for the fibers separating and look closely at an *E*'s teeth unpulping.

My brother Gary was the only one I could talk to.

For we are always

   the limbs

Gary.

Speech is Gary,
it shows.

Everything is
eyes, window glass,
lips, teeth,
metal signs
—they're Gary, quite Gary.

Cars are Gary.
Gray is Gary, gloves are Gary.
The road, robins,
all are Gary,
everything is and everyone is
out of luck who lives here.

When my sister Jill was born I remember her arms and legs spelling endlessly. She looked like every letter at once.

The history of *J* is motion shaped by *I*. The pinky finger pulling the optic nerve, forming a contrail over the short curl of my mother and sister. How could I say their names otherwise? A Judy-Jill song for the color of any morning.

I once caught a snake and held it as close to the point of nothingness as possible. It spiraled in the air: a letter bending toward me. What thought created its consonant? Strung such scales together only to tatter? Could such a contortion be its namesake? Was the word *snake* drawn purely from shape? Its sound? Or all of it at once? The curves combing a repeating letter in the grass until revealing on concrete. Did it also account for this town? Its drooping tree lines and slow bite? Saginaw?

Saginaw is sadder than I am able. The city shifts on the color of its
memory. Around me the fields are thick with ice and the colors of
ice, thawing of motors, work, sounds fall. One idles. In the cut of
the cold you could shatter. Out there lies the library veiled and lost
in letters. It all muddles. The whole riverside down to the water is
industry; it sags in the smoky air over streets lined with mailboxes:
48601, 48602, 48603. Birds bearing some yet-to-be color sing
faintly under another sun, someone else's sense of undenied light.

I would watch my father talk to himself, dust vacillating, his hands
slicing through, setting everything into a different motion. He made
lists in the air. I could see the transparency of the water bill, fear
of losing his welding job, thoughts on the new USPS application.
Bill signed, "Tell him," and how the post office clerk wrote *DEAF*
with a thick marker before tossing it in the pile. I was often locked
out of the house, would bend the storm screen back to get through.
Once he asked if I broke it. I snapped an *N* through my fingers and
watched him stomp into the kitchen.

Q bulbs from a factory spire. The billow compounds my vapor and forms hypnotically. Everything licked with the silver curl of a ghostly letter and must, of course, move opaquely so with everything else. Sometimes, especially on overcast days, no matter where, I feel the place. The non-heroic belt of slow fields churning in a microcosm, in which a light dulls, grating and the color of grating. Over it all drift clouds like great manufacturing hands ready to pluck a life.

The doctor told me Bill had kidney disease. I turned to him and signed it. Turning back to the doctor I said, "I'm donating my kidney." The doctor wrote in his file. Bill tapped my shoulder and signed, "Say you what?"

When we got home I told Judy. Her fingers bent and plowed the air in front of her face.

I could hear Judy getting home from work. I would stare at the flip clock. The motorized cylinder churns two camps of circles in small draws by way of a reduction gear: the dasher at a ratio of one revolution for each hour, the plodder at one for every twenty-four. It is 1:28 a.m. and the wheels move gently, the faster disk connected to an ecliptic of sixty plastic leaves. I stick my finger in the clock to force two neighboring leaves open—they spill a verse. Dropping a leaf increases the dream by one. The book flips vertically, its sheets blearing a memory. One page falls each minute to reveal a new digit. The slower disk bridges a similar fall of leaves, only there are forty-eight. These leaves have hour numbers: two for each numeral to represent absence or presence. One leaf weakens every thirty minutes, at 25 and 55. Minute leaves 45 through 59 have a small stem. At forty-five minutes past, you can hear the stem loose a branch that depresses into the hour wheel realm, catching a falling *L* at its proper time.

In some little gray thought I recognized a green idea that had not occurred before: Leave. It lulled through the expanse of an index finger and thumb, actualizing in a drive around the outer rim of town toward the expressway. Cornfields erasing what's already been erased, burning the shape of the sun after you look away.

& work the letters by hand, & refrain, & writhe an *I* until the graphite bonds, & write in the dark to let the lack pencil itself in, & let things be only because they are, & flesh them out.

& put to an end. & move out of the glassy roll, & break from an absence of noise. And not care for a bland thing, and be short of a version I no longer want, and be one kidney away from never leaving, and be a river, a god, and be almost forgotten. & imagine where nothingness comes, & imagine, & learn Chinese or any lucky number, & know the way a flat cut severs, & feel the metal wheels strain against rails, & hear an epiphany of trumpets out of tune, & bend a paperclip into a perfect line, & take the perfection and guide it into electricity.

& could have been a blur of knuckles filtered by a desire to multiply zero. I felt like an in-between. & is I, a twenty-seventh letter, some corrupted symbol of a boy's finger hovering over a map, measuring omission from one vaporous morning to the next, everything handed down, Bill and Judy piecing it all together somehow. I could have been a reflection if I stayed: mirroring

———————

Samuel Clare Knights was born and raised in Saginaw, Michigan. He holds a PhD in creative writing and literature from the University of Denver and an MFA from the Jack Kerouac School of Disembodied Poetics at Naropa University. He lives in Colorado and listens to the Grateful Dead every day.

EDITOR'S NOTE

Amy Sauber's "State Facts for the New Age" is a glimpse at a thirty-something schoolteacher's life unraveling after a breakup. For Bekah, newly single with only two cats and an amethyst-encrusted mat to keep her company, the middle school where she teaches is the stage on which, every day, the show must go on. Behind the scenes of Bekah half-assing geography lessons for eighth graders, we watch as the octopus arms of her contempt stretch toward her kooky therapist, closed-off ex, headmaster friend-but-boss, her students, and mostly herself. Sauber expertly captures the ambivalence of this contempt both with Bekah's deadpan observations ("A pigeon pancakes into the window and probably dies") and her increasing inability to hold the pieces of her life together in front of an audience of thirteen-year-olds.

As fiction editor for *The Rumpus*, I love finding and sharing stories that crack open ideas about the many identities that women can possess. What I love about Bekah is that she is not simply sad about being dumped; she's furious, and has no idea what to do with that fury. She is also negotiating shame, something Sauber captures in remarkable images: Bekah taking a knife to her expensive therapy mat; Bekah sitting on the floor of her classroom, sewing together the map she accidentally tore down the middle. This story is smart, painful, and funny—a moving debut.

Sarah Lyn Rogers, fiction editor
The Rumpus

STATE FACTS
FOR THE NEW AGE

Amy Sauber

DR. HURA IS a therapist I will never see again. I know this, sitting cross-legged on her couch, as she recommends a BioMat, a long electronic mat about half the length of a twin bed with crushed-up amethyst crystals inside a series of horizontal ridges.

"I'm not sure that's right," I say.

I've been talking at length about Micah, how our relationship is finished after six years. It seems like a stupid thing to see a therapist about. I try to compensate with research, symptom listing—a more concrete reason. I had confirmed on the internet that I might be depressed, have fibromyalgia or cancer, a brain metastasis. Web-diagnosis led me to Dr. Hura, but I don't tell her this part.

She flips over my forms and gently closes my file. Dr. Hura's hair is dark, with the exception of a skunk stripe sweeping through it. Her skin is icy, translucent, almost blue. She interlaces her skeletal hands, long and knobby, and rests them awkwardly high on her chest.

"You, Bekah, are here because you hurt," she says, and coughs, but weakly, almost like a giggle.

"I'm a shock absorber for tragedy," I say, not really knowing what I mean. "Maybe I should just move to Hawaii. I hear that's a happy place to live."

Dr. Hura listens, coughs or giggles, and says, "All right."

A Zen garden rests on a glass table. I use the miniature rake to draw seismographic patterns in the sand. There are stones with words on them. *Love. Hope. Peace.* I turn them all over.

"So what do you do with it? This BioMat," I say.

Dr. Hura rises and tiptoes to a massage table topped with a few pillows, presumably with the BioMat underneath. She reaches over and hands me a small throw pillow with beige and cream tassels. It is surprisingly hot. I join her at the mat.

"You lie on it, for about twenty to thirty minutes each day, absorbing the infrared heat," she says. "Turn the volume up if you are sick."

"The volume?"

"The dial. You turn it up when you are sick. More heat will kill the viruses."

I'm not sure I know what we are talking about anymore. She motions with a dial, left and right. There are tiny notches and temperature markings that range from 50 to 155 degrees. I look around her office, holding the pillow to my chest. Mason jars full of puzzle pieces line the bookshelf, neighbored by a few coffee table books about astrology, swimming pools, and blue-green algae.

"And this is going to help me?"

She furrows her bleached eyebrows and pulls her lips inward. For a moment I think she might cry.

"This will help you."

I think about the last thing Micah said to me: *You are a dark woman.*

I put the BioMat on my credit card and Dr. Hura namastes

goodbye. There is a strong probability that paying it off will take some time. I'm not even sure if the BioMat is legal. The thing comes packaged in a black suitcase that I wheel out to my clunker junker of a Honda. The sky is ominous with thunderstorm. I wonder if it will actually break. I slide the BioMat sideways into the backseat. I realize I've forgotten to give Dr. Hura back her throw pillow, which is now neither hot nor cold.

I TEACH GEOGRAPHY to eighth graders at Bridge Academy, which isn't the best school but not the worst. It's a small school, a brick building with blue castle-like towers, next to the crosstown. Dull light comes in from the back of my classroom on this grayish February day. Outside we hear honking and a fender bender. It smells like erasers and stale cotton candy.

We're doing a one-week unit on the U.S. and state facts. I point to South Dakota on the large vinyl map and drag my finger down, resting on a pastel yellow Texas.

"These are the tricky ones," I tell them.

It's a Tuesday and that means we have geography last period. Right now we're spending time memorizing what color is what state. I know if South Dakota isn't blue on the test, they'll be screwed.

"Think South Dakota: big and blue." I know this is not teaching.

They give me their zombie faces. A flock of white ibises flies by my window. Kristi splits her split ends with her teeth. South Dakota will be blue indefinitely and no amount of enthusiasm or adrenaline injections in the world can spring these last thirty minutes to life.

I tell them spelling, memorization tricks for each state. The chalk breaks as I write on the board, *Connect-i-cut*. I stand back, looking at my prison handwriting. I decide to switch gears and quiz them.

Jeff says, "Pier-ee."

Kristi says, "The capital of Washington is Olympics."

I pass out their notecards with their assigned states. Assignment: They each have two states—I've claimed home, the Carolinas—and they have to identify state flowers, birds, mottoes, and interesting facts. They give a notecard presentation, write a two-page paper. They complain—moaning, echoing their favorite word, *lame*, dropping their heads to their desks—because they all want California. I'm pretty sure all my students have never left South Carolina, so I don't know what they think they know about California. And then there's Jazzerie, who loves school more than anything in life. I don't have to worry about her. She is my best and most annoying student—annoying as of late, because I cannot tolerate her enthusiasm. I can hear her squealing over Rhode Island and Alaska as if she now owns them, the ones she's always wanted.

Durrell frowns at his notecard. He flips it over as if there has been some mistake.

"How do I do a report on Nebraska if nobody lives there?" he says, flapping the notecard against his desk.

"Oh, people live there," I say.

"How? They don't even have a football team."

"What's really wrong with Nebraska?" This comes out too aggressively. I know better than to ask these kinds of questions.

"Everything," Durrell says, carefully enunciating extra syllables.

Actually, it was Micah's idea to have them work on state facts. Two weeks ago, we'd sat on stools on the back porch, passing a hand-rolled cigarette back and forth. Micah had agreed with irrational tranquillity that he would be moving out with all his paintings and that I would keep the cats. This was decided, and it seemed like enough for one night, that we would talk more later. We never did. It was late, the porch light dimmed. The way the shadows fell, I could see only his hand in the dark, sort of floating, as it reached toward me for the cigarette.

"Didn't you ever have to learn the state song?" he said. His voice seemed to come from nowhere. "Alabama, Alaska, Arizona, Arkansas," he sang to the tune of "Turkey in the Straw."

"Never heard that song."

"You should try it."

"I'm not going to sing," I said. I thought, *How can you sing at a time like this?*

"Well, state facts could be good. Did you know that J. C. Penney was founded in Wyoming?"

"This is too hard."

But he just said, "Well, you are a dark woman."

I let my kids out early. I'm not allowed to do this, but it's only ten minutes. I tell them to be quiet, like bunnies, or moths or something.

Jazzerie whispers to me on the way out, "I have the largest and smallest states." She smiles. She has those clear braces but with blue rubber bands on the brackets. She's pretty popular despite these braces, one of the richest girls at school. The zippers of my students' backpacks tinkle down the hall.

AT HOME, I lie on the BioMat and stare up at the wood grain on my ceiling. I try to see patterns or faces or shapes, something Micah would do. I slide my hand under my underwear, then give up.

"In the future," I tell myself, but I don't finish my sentence. My clothes are smushed to one side of the closet. On the walls, a few nails stick out like warts.

Martha, the dumb cat, hops up on the bed. She tumbles onto her back, legs flopping awkwardly in the air. Dr. Sarah DeMint, the middle school headmaster, calls to see how I'm doing, talking quickly and nasally. Our weekly friends-but-she's-my-boss chat.

"How was that therapist? How are your students?"

I tell her about the BioMat. "It's like radiation rock therapy," I say.

"Is that safe? Are you sure you went to a therapist?"

I explain how it works and rifle through the bedside drawer next to me. It's jammed full of randomness. One of Durrell's old homework assignments, a stuffed monkey Micah bought me one birthday, a lone earring, a rusted screwdriver, a Byrds CD.

Sarah stalls for moment, making a weird clicking sound with her tongue. "Huh," she says. "Different." She changes the subject to how it's going without Micah, which I find annoying.

"Fine. It's not much different," I say. This is not a complete lie. Basically, I've been going without Micah for a while. It's just that now he has all his stuff.

I shove the monkey farther back in the drawer, as if it will dry up and die back there. I snap the Byrds CD in half. We hang up, and I look up facts about North and South Carolina on my phone, recording them on the back of Durrell's old homework that I've ripped up into notecards. I discover that the state mineral for South Carolina is the amethyst and take this as a sign. I tell myself that maybe the BioMat is like one of those pills that has to build up in your system.

I roll over onto my stomach. My back feels roasted. The mat gives off deep heat, like body heat. I sort of hug it. I fall asleep and have terrible dreams with terrible repetitive music, a mixture between a hymn and a circus jingle. *Here we have Idaho. Here we have Idaho.* When I wake up, the lights are still on. It is too early in the morning, and the BioMat has shut itself off.

IT'S ONE OF those freak days where the temperature is up near eighty, and I'm wearing the wrong clothes.

Bridge Academy is decorated with red, pink, and white heart garlands, and everyone is high on chocolate. Since Tuesday, Durrell has made six tiny crane birds from aluminum candy wrappers. I find them carefully balanced on all the chalk. The art teacher hangs sixth grader Twizzler portraits near my classroom. Lots of people with Twizzler hair that won't stay glued down and sprout off the white cardboard. Very Raggedy Ann. I nearly overdose on conversation hearts.

Students and teachers send carnations to each other, an annual event this time of year. The flowers are delivered to kids' lockers and to classrooms. I receive two. One from Dr. Sarah DeMint, and one from Anonymous with a note in Durrell's noodley cursive. "Roses are red, South Dakota is blue, here is a NY State fact for you: New York invented the toilet in 1857."

Before lunch, Dr. Sarah DeMint and I meet about how my quarter is going, and I slip up, forgetting she's my boss, and tell her that Jazzerie is a princess bitch and Kristi Collins might be the dumbest student I've ever had. I go on when I know I shouldn't about how Durrell is assaulting me with Valentines.

"It's sexual harassment," I say.

"Durrell is twelve," she says. "I'm going to pretend that you didn't just say that." She scribbles something in my file.

In geography, a pigeon pancakes into the window and probably dies. Also, I accidentally rip the map.

"Kansas isn't just *Wizard of Oz* stuff," I say.

I look down and see the piece of chalk that made me lose my footing and subsequently stab the country with my meter stick, right across Kansas and into Colorado, Utah. Durrell and his buddies laugh.

Jazzerie gasps. "Oh, the heartland!"

I mat back some sweaty hair behind my ear. "How about the state song?"

The bell rings, I grade, school ends. After the last bell, I resolve to stitch up the gash and search through my drawer for adhesives. I find rubber cement and a small thread mending kit from a Folly Beach Marriott, located twenty minutes away, a vacation Micah and I once took after he sold one of his large paintings. This mending involves unhinging the map from the pulley and pushing back all the front-row desks so I can lay the map flat on the floor. The vinyl gash has already begun to fray. The school is quiet and I spend a long time tracing rivers until they evaporate into other states.

Dr. Sarah DeMint pokes her head through the door. "Damnit, we just bought those," she says, arms crossed, head shaking. "Let me guess, Durrell Walkins." But this is an act. I can tell by the way she inhales that there is more she wants to say, but she doesn't.

I go home and I lie on the BioMat for hours, much longer than recommended. My amethyst radiation. I try to burrito my head inside it, pretending that I am a superhero being recharged even though this is bullshit. Peeling back the quilted covering, I watch the rocks at work. For some reason, I expect them to glow, but they just look like purple rocks. The mat is making me so dehydrated I'm peeing ochre.

Julia, the bitchy cat, scratches at a bolster pillow, shaving velour fuzz everywhere.

"Stop it. Just stop it," I say, and Julia hisses. "You could've gone with him, for christsake."

When I think about Micah, I think about things I wish I could forget. We're on the beach, my head in Micah's lap. My sundress pulled up over my face, Micah pulls away from me to sketch. It is stupid.

I think back to something Dr. Hura said in our only meeting. She stood up, took her X-rayish hands, palms up, and opened her arms wide as if she were moving into a yogic pose.

"Attachment only leads to suffering," she warned.

I get off the mat and unplug it from the wall. In the kitchen, I rummage in the drawer for the dull steak knife. Row by row, I split open the BioMat, collecting the amethysts in the skirt of my dress. They are still warm. I dump the rocks into a pile in the empty side of the closet.

Dr. Hura got it wrong. Maybe I just need something cold, like Fla-Vor-Ice or sorbet.

I drive out to the Harris Teeter around the corner. I smile at a young couple pushing a stroller. I let an older woman take the last basket and enjoy a free sample of grapes and cheddar. In the frozen foods, Micah holds hands with young woman. Blond, alabaster skin. I try not to look at her face. Or his face, anyone's face. There is a loud screeching in my mind. I turn and run, knocking over a large bread display and slipping on plastic. I get up and abandon a carton of raspberry sorbet with the bananas. I'm not sure if I am breathing. I speed through two stop signs and when I get home, I swing open the door and lock it behind me. I kick over the cats' food dishes. I strip off my leggings and kick them off and peel off

my dress and hang it sloppily on the doorknob and click on the
BioMat. Except I forgot that I just ripped it apart. I stare at the rock
spectrum in my closet and kick that, too.

When I reach my hand into my underwear, this time I cry.

I'M SEVEN MINUTES late for geography. They are supposed to
start their presentations today. I run in sweating and panting and
slam the door behind me. My button-up shirt is inside out. Durrell
is standing up to leave, swinging his backpack around his shoulder.
When he sees me, he sits back down in his seat, slowly, with his
backpack on. He looks at me strangely, as if I'm not his geography
teacher or anyone he knows at all. I pull down the U.S. map, making that unzipping sound. There's that wonky blister over Kansas,
Colorado, Utah.

Jazzerie shoots up her hand. "Can I go first?"

"Kristi, you're up," I say.

Kristi flinches. She rises automatically, tripping over her own
backpack, weaving her awkward way around desks to the front of
the classroom. She looks over to me as if she is pleading, tries to
speak to the class, and looks back over to me. I know this makes
me a bad person.

"Um, Virginia is a state for lovers," she begins.

"You know what, Kristi, on second thought, why don't you go
on Monday," I say, fanning myself with a book.

"I-I can do this," she stammers.

"Nope. You know, today is not a day for Virginia. You can go
on Monday. It's fine. It'll be better this way," I say. "Jazzerie, if you
want to go, the time is now."

"It's just what I found in my research," Kristi says.

"Jazz-er-ie."

Kristi jangles some brass bracelets on her wrist. She looks as if she might cry. I tell myself she is not upset, just confused. A pencil drops to the floor. The heat clicks on, for some stupid reason, and blows stale hot breath on my neck.

Jazzerie confidently sashays up to the front of the classroom. It is like she was born to give this presentation. She flicks back her ponytail with her hand. Standing with her legs apart, she pulls out a thick stack of notecards from her jeans pocket. She reads swiftly, her nose tilted up toward the class.

"I have Alaska, the largest state, and Rhode Island, the smallest. They are opposites. Rhode Island is cute and tiny and way over here and its state bird is the domesticated red chicken. While Alaska is like the Hulk on steroids, way over there. In fact, Rhode Island can fit in Alaska over four hundred twenty times. Alaska is America's Last Frontier. Its state bird is the willow ptarmigan, which is kind of like a chicken, but it's not. And the state flower is the forget-me-not, a blue flower, a flower of remembrance, often worn by ladies as a sign of faithfulness and everlasting love."

"Enough. Pens and paper," I say, standing up from my desk. They know this means they need to write this down, that a quiz may be looming.

Jazzerie protests, "But I just started my—"

"Jazzerie, sit down now."

And she does, but not before she gives me her jaw-swinging braces bitch face. From my blazer pocket, I whip out my homemade notecards, more prison scrawl and smudged pen.

I begin. "North Carolina is this green state. Here. Capital, Raleigh. The Wright brothers flew the first plane at Kitty Hawk. Look at this: mountains, piedmont, coast. North Carolina sandwich.

The Tar Heel State. Home of the Panthers. The cardinal is the state bird and the state flower is the dogwood. North Carolina's state motto is 'To be, rather than to seem.' And you should always be someone you *are* and never *seem* like someone that you will never be. Because seeming is lying. It is cheating, plagiarism. And that's all you need to know about North Carolina. Oh, and that Andrew Jackson, the seventh president, was born there in Waxhaw. And did you know that Andrew Jackson's wife died of stress because he was obsessed with winning the election? This is what happens when your whole life revolves around someone else and their elitist life goals."

My students look up at me and back down, their pens and pencils furiously scribbling. I pause. Jeff peers over to Jazzerie to cheat off her notes. They whisper about something and giggle. Flirting probably. Flirting in my class like little shitstorms.

"He killed his wife?" Durrell says. He rubs his head with his eraser. "In North Carolina?"

"South Carolina," I say loudly. Loudly enough for the whole room to quiet and everyone to stop writing. Light filters into the classroom at a sharp angle and the tops of my students' heads light up for a second before it slips behind some clouds. "The Palmetto State. Back in the day, people made palmetto cabbage from the trees, and you bet that it tasted like boiled vomit. They never could cook, but what's worse is that they never even tried. Trees don't taste good. There is enough real food here to satisfy a nation, and they were lazy. South Carolina: the first to secede from the Union. Launch of the Civil War, which wasn't civil at all, which is good. You should never have civil breakups. And if you do have a civil breakup, don't get left behind with the cats and the apartment. You don't want these things, believe me. Don't buy an electrified rock mat at the recommendation of your therapist. It won't bring you peace of mind. Columbia is the capital. State bird: Carolina wren. State flower: yellow jasmine. See that? It's yellow on the map. Yellow state, yellow jasmine."

I know I'm going down the train track to hell, but I can't stop myself.

"'*In South Carolina there are many tall pines*' is the beginning of a Gram Parsons song that you've probably never heard because you're thirteen, but this is not a song I ever want to hear again, especially in the morning on a foggy day when I'm feeding seagulls a lasagna dinner that was never eaten. South Carolina has several attractions as a tourist destination. For instance, Middleton Place is a damn Southern castle. Have you been to the beach? Dolphins, guaranteed. Which is why South of the Border is never a place where you take your girlfriend, never, especially not on her thirtieth birthday. Not even for art. Do not take your girlfriend to a campy tourist mecca with a thirty-foot sombrero-hatted neon-lit tower. After all this time, you should know her better. And if you happen to do this, you do not say, *Isn't this funny? Isn't this fascinating?* as a way to make up for the fact you are stalled here for a good three hours because someone needs to dick off doing some kind of art thing on South of the Border."

Jazzerie's hand springs up. "But I love South of the Border."

"Why would a person like that place?"

"Because it's fun. And they have really good popcorn and you can pet donkeys and stuff."

We glare at each other. In my mind, Jazzerie is being thrown out the window by a blown-up cardboard version of South Carolina, thrown to a muddy pickup truck that will take her far, far away from here. She begins to talk again, but I overpower her.

"South Carolina is a very important state," I yell, clapping my hands together. I wonder, briefly, if I could be suspended. I flip wildly through my notecards, toss some to the floor. My students have stopped writing entirely. I gasp for breath. "South Carolina has a motto, '*Dum spiro spero*,' which means 'While I breathe, I hope.' And couldn't we all use a little hope these days? Right? State shell: the lettered olive. The Riverdogs are our minor league baseball team, but don't fall in love at baseball games because it's probably a curse. And lastly, the state mineral of South Carolina is the amethyst, which is used to heal people who hurt, especially in February, because it is February."

Crying in front of eighth graders is a new low point in my life. I can't even look at them. All my notecards fallen, splayed out all over the floor. Bless America, shit.

I stumble to a cold metal chair off to the left of the blackboard. I drip liquid snot. When I finally look up, they are all staring at me. Horrified, contorted, tearful faces. There are only the faint sounds from outside, a little buzz of traffic. We sit like this for some time before I call on Durrell.

Durrell, backpack still strapped, carries a two-gallon cooler to the front of the class and rests it on my desk. He pulls out a sleeve of Dixie cups from his backpack and untwists the tie. Carefully, he rests the cups on the chalk rest of the chalkboard, then changes his mind and sets them quietly on my desk. He leans back from me, pouring a small cup of red juice that smells like syrup. His hands are dry and small, even for a thirteen year-old. He sets the cup in front of me; the red substance sways, then calms. He doesn't dare look me in the eye.

Two, three cups at a time, he fills them halfway and hands them out to the class by rows. Somehow they automatically know to pass the little cups back so everyone can have one. He is careful not to step on my fallen notecards, only nudging a few with the tip of his Air Jordans.

"Nebraska was my first state. Edwin Perkins invented Kool-Aid in Nebraska in 1927," Durrell says. Durrell talks about meadow-larks and corn before he starts his report about New York, but I'm not really able to listen. He even makes the class laugh about something I don't hear because I'm trying to focus intently on the Kool-Aid Dixie cup disintegrating on my planner. I'm only able to stare at this sample size of Kool-Aid. I pick it up and take a sip, knowing it will stain my teeth.

At the end of class, I tell them I'll see them Monday, when the rest of their state projects are due. I tell them they all get A's for the day, as some kind of coded desperate bribe. They file out. Jazzerie flies past me, Jeff chasing after her. Kristi gives me a half smile then war-paths. Durrell tells me to try to relax this weekend. He tells me his older brother freaks out sometimes and nods as if I'm supposed to understand what this means. I assume it's not good.

The sun shines in that strange angle where all the dust lights up, swirling and twinkling. I could be slipping into another di-mension. Maybe if I try, I'll end up some place far away, like Nebraska or Iowa, or, better yet, Alaska. Of course, this doesn't work. They won't turn in their projects Monday. They can't. It's Presidents' Day and there is no school.

THE FOLLOWING WEEK I ask to take a temporary leave of absence.

"Two weeks," Dr. Sarah DeMint says, relieved, "should give you a little regroup time."

After our meeting, I drive my clunker junker down 17-South as if I'm going to Savannah, through some forests and marshes, past some white-tailed deer gathering by the side of the road. The highway becomes two lanes. I make a sudden turn, onto the connector to Edisto Island, and am reminded how much Micah enjoyed this drive. He loved it because he thought it was like going into space above the green marshland, stretching endlessly.

I pull over here on the connector and get out. Every now and then, a car zooms past. I planned to drop my amethysts and homespun notecards over the bridge, but I decide against it. Actually, I'm not sure why I drove out here. When I made the turn, I thought I might break down, but I think it's all out now.

I look out into the space of the land, the air cool and nipping at the exposed space between my cropped pants and my socks. The color of the water seems to match the grayness in the sky. Marsh grass has faded to a rusty wheat. There is a flock of geese off toward the horizon. A few ibises, like little white specks, flutter and disappear into the grass. From somewhere there is a whiff of detritus and pluff mud. I take a deep breath and get back into my car and drive home.

To my surprise, I receive a letter in the mail a few days later. It's from my geography class. How could they want anything to do with me, ever again? *Get Well Soon*, it says with all their scrawly middle school signatures and a few state mottoes.

Durrell writes that Oregon's state motto is "She flies with her own wings." He says, "Be a bird, Ms. R. (And that wasn't even my state!)"

Kristi says, "New Hampshire says, 'Live free or die!'"

There are a few others: "I have found it"; "To the stars through adversity"; "Ever upward"; "It grows as it goes; Eureka!"

I make a little pin prick near the top of the fold in the card. I pin it with a nail to my wall, fold my arms and stand back.

Amy Sauber lives in New Hampshire, where she is working on a collection of short stories. From the Carolinas, she holds an MFA from the University of New Hampshire and currently teaches in Maine.

EDITOR'S NOTE

"The Asphodel Meadow" stood out from the very beginning, both in terms of style and subject matter. With its minimalistic, matter-of-fact sentences and its way of introducing the premise with just the right amount of ambiguity and feeling, the story quickly became an interesting and entertaining read. We're suckers for engaging first-person narratives, and especially those that make us empathize with the protagonist and root for the underdog, regardless of whether the eventual outcome is ever disclosed and without having complete details of the entire situation. Another notable characteristic of the story is the way it uses repeated words and phrases. For us, 99 percent of the time we see repeated words, we wince and cringe, but in this piece the repetition works.

Joseph Levens, editor
The Summerset Review

THE ASPHODEL MEADOW

Jim Cole

HE INVITED MY wife to hike up a mountain. She laughed. She twisted her hair in a tight bun. He stepped out onto the porch and picked up the morning newspaper. The air was cool. Dew covered the buttercups. He put the roof down on his sports car. A neighbor peeked through the curtains. Lamb's wool covered the car seats. My wife put on her shorts. She pulled a pink T-shirt over her black bra. She slipped her feet into white sandals. She nestled in the sheepskin. He handed her the newspaper. She dropped it on the floorboard.

She turned to him and said, "*Look at what passes for the new. You will not find it there but in despised poems.*"

She pushed her feet against the dashboard and stroked black polish on her toenails. "Don't hit any fucking bumps," she said.

He dropped a backpack behind her seat. Inside the backpack there was a bottle of water and a map and a bag of almonds and a pomegranate and a pocketknife.

"Don't fucking drip on my upholstery," he said.

He turned the key in the ignition and they headed toward the mountain.

✦

MY WIFE IS a poet. Four years ago, a publisher accepted her first book. We were on our honeymoon. We were camping in an orange tent. I woke in the sleeping bag the second morning and the light inside the tent was orange, and my wife was gone. The tent flap was open. I looked up and stared at a mosquito on the ceiling.

THEY LISTENED TO traffic reports and jazz. He drove fast on the highway out of the city. He drove down a dirt road and over a wooden bridge. He parked the car in a meadow that had tall grass and lilies and cows. The cows turned their heads and they looked at my wife.

He got out of the car. He unfolded the map. He spread the map on the hood. The hood of the car was hot. On the map it said the top of the mountain was 1,044 feet above sea level. My wife opened her car door. He spread the map in the dirt. My wife put her feet on the corners of the map and looked. He kneeled down and he put his thumb on a spot on the map that read, 1,044 FT. He stretched out his hand and he put his little finger near my wife's left foot.

He said, "That's how far we have to go. How far do you think it is from there to there?"

He held up his hand and stared from his thumb to his little finger. His knees were dirty.

"Annie," he said, "that's where we are going. A beautiful meadow full of flowers. Hot as hell, but filled with flowers. Drink water. It'll be hot as hell. Stay hydrated."

She said, *"I was cheered when I came first to know that there were flowers also in hell."*

✦

THE SECOND MORNING of my honeymoon, the air in the tent was cold. My eyesight was blurry. I looked around the tent. I took a sip of water from a plastic bottle. I peeked outside. Three elk walked by.

MY WIFE STARTED to hike up the trail. The trail was in the woods. They walked in the shade. They saw poison oak. They saw ferns. They saw three banana slugs. They saw spider webs. They looked at trees lying on the ground. Those trees were dead. The ground was soft. He stopped to pee and saw orange mushrooms. My wife saw a black caterpillar. He took off his shoes and his socks. He walked in the mud. His toes were muddy. He said, "Take off your sandals."

"My nails. They're going to get muddy," my wife said. She asked him if the ground felt chilly. She said she was afraid of banana slugs. She smiled.

They walked beside a stream. He carried my wife's sandals in the backpack. They saw a cluster of forget-me-nots. He said if he tried to pick them for her, he would fall in the water. She laughed. She said she would like to see that.

"That's the German legend," he said. "The girl's lover dies drowning. You know I can't swim, right?"

"Maybe I would save you," my wife said.

My wife picked four blackberries. He pointed to acorns on the trail. He pointed at hoofprints on the trail. He said they were from unicorns. He walked beside my wife where the trail widened. He said maybe she could capture a unicorn.

She sat on a log. Her toes were muddy. He rubbed the mud off her feet. He slipped her feet into her sandals.

They walked out of the woods. They were on the top of the mountain. My wife saw two praying mantises. They did not move. They were the color of the grass. She saw a lizard on a rock. She saw another praying mantis.

My wife pointed at the lizard and she said, "Look at that. How did it lose its tail?"

He said, "Maybe his lover bit it off."

"No," she said, "that's praying mantises. And it's their heads."

He saw two praying mantises beside a stream. One was eating a fly.

He said, "Why are there so many fucking praying mantises?"

THAT MORNING ON my honeymoon, I found my wife sitting in a green truck with a park ranger. I walked to the truck. I had on boxers and wool socks. Pine needles stuck to my socks.

"They called," she said through the windshield. She made a fist against her cheek and held out her thumb and little finger. She opened the door. "They called. They found me all the way out here."

I said, "You left me."

She had on my gray sweatpants and a pair of sandals.

"The ranger knocked on the tent door," she said. "He said I had a phone call. A call from New York. All the way out here. It must have been nine o'clock there. They accepted my collection, and they found me. Who knows how they found me?"

THEY STEPPED OVER the stream. They came to the meadow. The meadow was filled with yellow asphodel.

My wife walked in the field. Four vultures flew in a circle. There was a breeze and the flowers swayed. Across the meadow there was a barn with no roof, and there was a burned-out school bus. He walked behind her. She stopped and she told him to turn around. She opened the backpack. She removed the knife.

She leaned down and grasped the stem of a flower. The stalk was thick and hard as wood. She cut it. She cut two more. My wife sat down.

WE PACKED THE tent and we reached the airport at sunset. I put her bags on the curb.

"This is what it's like to be married to a creative type," she said. She smiled. A policewoman blew a whistle and waved at me. My wife picked up her bags and she kissed me. She smelled like the campfire.

I fastened the seat belt. I phoned my manager and I said if he needed me to work the next day, I could.

MY WIFE SPREAD the asphodels across her lap. He stood behind my wife and he stared at her pink T-shirt. He looked at the sweat on her neck.

He took off his shirt. My wife turned her head and she looked at him. She smiled. She turned back and gazed across the field. He unbuttoned his shorts. She looked up at the vultures. He took off his tennis shoes. He took off his socks. The dry grass jabbed his feet and ankles. Rocks poked the soles of his feet.

He unzipped his shorts. He pushed them and his boxers to his ankles. He stepped out of his shorts and boxers, and he put them on top of his tennis shoes. He bent down and put his T-shirt on top. He stared at my wife, and sweat rolled down his body.

She said, "What are you doing?"

He said, "I told you it would be hot as hell."

"Seriously. What are you doing?"

"What does it look like?"

He put his hands on his hips. She stared at him. The sun was on his back. A breeze blew between his legs.

She said he was naked and he was being bad. She asked what if someone saw.

He told my wife, "Take off your clothes."

She said, "No."

He looked up, and the vultures flew in circles. He stepped over my wife's legs. He straddled her legs and looked down on her. She tugged on her hair, and her hair fell down on her shoulders. She leaned back on her elbows.

He told my wife to cut the pomegranate because he wanted it.

She handed him half the fruit, and the juice ran down her arm. It dripped off her elbow. He scraped out the seeds with his fingers. The juice dripped off his wrists. It dripped on his foot. He handed her the seeds, and my wife ate them.

He told my wife to take her clothes off.

She looked up at him. She took off the T-shirt. She removed the black bra.

He said there was not a soul in the meadow. He kneeled down. He removed the asphodels from her lap. He unsnapped her shorts. He slipped my wife's feet out of her sandals. He kissed her toes. He unzipped her shorts. He kissed her stomach. She arched her back and he tugged on her shorts and her underpants. He tugged again. She wriggled. He put her sandals and T-shirt and bra and shorts and underpants in a pile. My wife was naked in the flowery field. He kissed my wife's breasts. He moved his fingers up and down her legs. He pressed his thumb in her bellybutton. He spread out his hand and he stretched his little finger down between my wife's legs.

He said, "How far is it from there to there?"

He pressed his body against my wife's body. The sun was hot. She closed her eyes.

He kissed her lips. He put his knee between her legs. There was a helicopter. He pushed his thigh against her. She opened her eyes. She put her hand to her forehead and shielded her eyes. Sweat dripped off his earlobe and it landed on her cheek. The sound of the helicopter blades got louder. The helicopter was yellow and it had the number 714 on the tail. She closed her eyes. She spread her legs. He stopped moving.

"We can pretend we are dead," he whispered.

They lay still in the grass. The helicopter flew in circles. The thumping sound moved away. My wife opened her eyes. They laughed.

He pressed his toes in the dry grass. She raised her knees. His toes dug down in the black dirt. His knees rubbed against the dry grass. The helicopter returned. My wife listened to it come closer. He rested his head on her shoulder.

He said, "Why is there so much fucking air traffic?"

He stopped moving and he closed his eyes. My wife closed her eyes. They listened to it go away. They did not move. He and my wife pretended together that they were dead.

He dug his toes in the dirt. He clutched clumps of grass. The grass tore. He grabbed onto more grass. He growled and my wife smiled. He looked at my wife's face. She turned her face to one side. She was smiling. She looked at a praying mantis. She stared at the asphodels. They swayed in the breeze. In the asphodel meadow my wife was naked, and she was with him, and she was perfectly happy.

———————

Jim Cole is a writer in Northern California with a rhetoric degree from University of California Berkeley and an MFA from the University of San Francisco, where his work was nominated for the AWP Intro Journals Project. He lives in the town of Duncans Mills, on the Russian River.

EDITOR'S NOTE

We've all heard the adage that there's only two types of stories: a stranger comes to town, or man goes on a journey. In its own way, "Solee" by Crystal Hana Kim does both of these. A handsome stranger arrives at the home of Solee and her family; the way he treats the oldest daughter of the house, on the verge of her own womanhood, sets Solee on a voyage of self-discovery. One traveler moves through physical space, while the other departs on a journey of emotional growth—I was impressed by how Crystal handled both so deftly.

"Solee" also resonated with me as a reader of Southern literature. We have many aspects of the traditional Southern story: the small, isolated town; the precocious girl making her way in the world; the wondrous walks through the forest—there's even a swimming hole and a charming cur. These tropes are transposed onto an entirely different environment, that of rural Korea. In that way, the story does a lot to demonstrate the scope of what we do at *The Southern Review*—from our foundations in Southern letters, we've expanded our reach to celebrate a world of literature—and every so often, that world proves itself to be a small enough place that even a small town, halfway around the planet, looks familiar.

Now in our ninth decade, *The Southern Review* has built relationships with more than 3,000 writers. It would be easy enough for us, as editors, to rely on those proven contributors to fill every issue. But finding stories like "Solee" in the mail—Crystal actually mailed in this piece, manila envelope and all—keeps me excited for the new.

Emily Nemens, coeditor
The Southern Review

SOLEE

Crystal Hana Kim

I COUNT THE stray dog's ribs on my way to school. Five bones protrude, like the rounded claw of a Dokkaebi clutching his club. Last month, there were six showing through the skin of his belly. I am happy. I am fattening him up after all.

He walks alongside me every day, and at the school yard entrance I give him a treat. He is so hungry he leaves a puddle of drool in my palm. But today he is frightened by a thunderclap rumbling through the air.

A man on a motorcycle. Wheels licking up bursts of dust. He waves and smiles. I am the only one on the road.

As he disappears, I wave back.

I HEAR LAUGHTER before I take off my shoes. Daddy and Mommy in the kitchen, singing with the girls.

"Why is everyone so happy?" I ask.

"Come say hello to your uncle." Daddy hugs me with his good arm. He is in a rare light mood; alcohol already swims in his mouth.

With Jieun and Mila and Mommy is the man from the morning. There is dust on his face and his skin is dark, like the farmers in the fields.

"Kyunghwan, meet Solee. She's my oldest and smartest, like a boy."

I tug down my short hair. I hate it when Daddy calls me a boy. "You're the man on the motorcycle," I say.

"You're the girl who feeds the starving dog." He laughs. Everyone laughs.

Daddy tells me to go bow to him properly, but I stick my head into Mommy's soft stomach. She holds me, brushing my hair and letting my embarrassment drain out.

"Say hello like this!" Jieun stands on her chair, leans over Mila, and kisses the man on the cheek. Everyone laughs again.

He hugs me as though we know each other. His cheek is softer than Daddy's, and his breath smells like tea, even though they are all drinking makgeolli. "Hello, Miss Solee," he says.

They get drunk as if we girls are invisible. It's nice. Once, on Jieun's third birthday, Mommy and Daddy drank so much at dinner they stumbled out of the restaurant. They left us at the table, our hands sticky from rice cakes and sugar tea. In the doorway, they kissed. I hope they will do that again.

IT'S EARLY WHEN I wake up. I lie still, letting the cool of the floor collect inside me. It's my job to make tea in the morning. Jieun and Mila sleep with open mouths. I imagine dropping seeds down their throats, so the kernels will settle in their bellies and grow. Pear blossoms flowing out between their lips, crawling up the walls of the room. I could puppet them around by their stalks, have *them* get the tea.

I'm not the only one awake. Uncle is seated at the table with a book. Washed and brushed, he doesn't look like a farmer anymore. I stare at my feet. I am wearing my nightclothes decorated with small frogs. They are too short in the sleeves and at the ankles.

"Morning, Solee."

"Morning, Uncle."

"That makes me feel old. Do I look like an old man to you?"

"I don't know."

"Call me Kyunghwan." He points to the tea he has already made. The napkins are folded into flowers and tucked underneath each cup.

"I need to bring these to my parents," I say.

"They'll wake up soon. They can get their own tea. Come, sit." He nods at the seat across from him. He gives me an American cookie. It is rectangular and beige and patterned with small, square indents. The sweetness makes the back of my ears hurt. I decide he is a nice man after all.

"What are your plans for today, Miss Solee?"

"I have school, and then I come home and help Mommy."

"Jisoo says you could go to college. What subjects do you like?"

"Math is easy. Composition, because we get to write stories. Science, because we learn about animals and plants."

Kyunghwan quizzes me with addition and subtraction problems. I start to boast that I even know multiplication, but I stop. Mommy says girls should show their smarts, but no one likes a bragger. That's the reason the other school kids are not nice to me.

"What's your dog's name?"

I want to say something clever. "Dokkaebi."

Kyunghwan smiles. "Those gremlins gave me nightmares when I was your age." He tells me stories of Dokkaebis playing pranks on children and old men. He is a good storyteller, using his hands and baring his teeth in suspenseful moments. Soon it is seven o'clock. "I have to get dressed for school," I say.

"I'm going hiking this afternoon. Do you want to come along?" He nods, as if I have already said yes. "We'll buy you some sturdy shoes."

"Bye, Kyunghwan," I say, waving and bowing at the same time. I'm glad Jieun and Mila are still too young to make tea.

TEACHER HAN RAPS my knuckles twice during mathematics. He tells me to pay attention. This afternoon, I will walk up a mountain with Kyunghwan. I play with my hair, brushing it down with my fingers. I wish Mommy hadn't cut it short. Kyunghwan likes long hair. Last night during dinner, his eyes spiraled as Mommy twirled a long, loose strand.

After school, I play gonggi stones with my classmates and wait. Chunja is the best, throwing and catching quickly. She has her own set of stones, and they are smooth from all her hours of practice. I'm in the middle of catching the stones with the back of my hand when the talking starts.

"Look!"

"Who is he?"

"He looks like a movie star."

"Someone's daddy?"

"He's *handsome*," Chunja says.

The boys stare, too, pointing at his hairy legs and the big lump at his throat.

He calls my name, waving brown shoes. I drop the gonggi stones into Chunja's hand, smiling at her surprise.

✦

WE ARRIVE AT Gasan. Even before we start climbing, there are large stains underneath Kyunghwan's arms and around his neck. When the boys at school sweat, we make fun of them. But on him, it looks different.

"Movie star," I whisper, hoping he will hear me.

He names flowers and trees. I try to remember them all, but the words bleed together.

"You see this?" Kyunghwan points to a strange little plant with nubs that curl inward, like a ram's horns. "It's Haemi's favorite side dish. Gosari. Wouldn't it be nice if we picked some for her?" He sets his hand on my head.

"My favorite side dish is fried eggs rolled up," I say.

"Well, if you help me with this, I'll make my most delicious eggs especially for you. All right?"

I nod. He opens his canvas bag, making room in the middle. We search for Mommy's favorite plant. I pluck one and stare. It looks as if a fuzzy caterpillar is curling up on my palm, ready for sleep. I will not eat any of them, I decide.

As we collect, he explains that these are babies, that when they mature the leaves uncurl and bloom. When we have a big enough pile, we take a break. He lies down with his hands clasped behind his head, maybe drying his armpits. I copy him. He explains how we will dry the baby plants in the sun, dust them lightly with salt and oil, and then fry them over a fire.

"How did you know it was her favorite?"

"Haemi and I were friends. A long time ago. I introduced her to my cousin, Jisoo. And that's how you and your sisters got to be here."

It's funny how he calls them by their first names. I roll over. I pick a dandelion and blow white fluff at him. "Do you have any children?"

"I wish I could have daughters as lovely as you girls. I missed my chance. Now I'm old and ugly."

"I think you're handsome," I say. I turn my head to his chest, so he can't see my face.

WE HEAD TO the backyard and Kyunghwan finds the right spot for the gosari. Out of reach of the roof's and the tree's shadows, where the sun heats the ground all day. The back of my neck prickles, and I don't want to watch these plants shrivel up any longer. I kick at a mud clump while Kyunghwan works. He is spreading them out to make sure they dry evenly.

"I'm tired," I say. Dokkaebi is circling the tree and I whistle him over.

"We're almost done."

Dokkaebi snuffles his head into my hands.

"No food for you," I say. I break a dirt clump over his back, mixing brown into his yellow fur. "I'm tired," I say again. I know I'm whining, but I can't help it.

Kyunghwan looks up. "I'm sorry. I should have brought you home earlier." He pulls a handkerchief from his pocket. It is the color of boiled spinach. He dips it in a bucket of water and washes my face. From forehead to nose to chin. He is not tickling me, but it feels like he is.

He wraps the kerchief around my neck, and a trickle of water drips down to my belly. I follow the stain with my finger. "I want my special eggs now."

"Go inside and let Haemi know we're home. I'll finish here, then I'll cook you up something delicious. You can keep the handkerchief for being such a good partner today."

I run into the house with my head raised, so everyone can see what Kyunghwan has given me to keep. "Look!"

"My wood nymph." Mommy kisses me. "How was your hike with Uncle?"

"He picked some baby plants for you. He said they're your favorite and that you like to eat them with your mouth wide open. Like this." I copy Kyunghwan's chewing, smacking my tongue against the roof of my mouth.

Before I can start describing the peak and my new brown shoes and the eggs that I will get to eat, her eyes close.

"Mommy?" I shake her, trying to bring her back to me. She does this sometimes. "Kyunghwan is waiting for you."

She smiles slowly, like a goddess returning to her human body. She squeezes my hand. "Watch the girls while I talk to your uncle." Raking her fingers through her curls, she walks out.

IT HAS BECOME a game between the two of us. I get up earlier each day, but Kyunghwan always wins. He sits in the kitchen with the hot tea ready. As we wait for the others to wake up, we talk.

Jieun and Mila come next, always running to him with their orange blanket dragging behind them, like an open dress. He pulls them onto his lap and feeds them spoonfuls of tea. I want him to feed me too, but he winks and I straighten up. He thinks of me as a grown-up.

At night, though, when everyone has gone to bed, I imagine him hugging me. I want to see him, and when I sneak into the hallway no one stops me. No three-legged crow guarding the door from intruders, as Mommy tells us on nights full of shouts and stomps.

At his door I bend down, dusting my ear against the crack to listen for his breathing. I have to lie as still as possible, but then I hear it. The in and out of Kyunghwan asleep.

It is Kyunghwan's ninth day here and Daddy is in a good mood again. It is a Saturday, a no-school day for me, and Daddy is eating breakfast with us.

"Listen," he says. "When Kyunghwan and I were boys, he found a secret pond."

"Where the air tastes sweet and the water is clear!" Kyunghwan sings.

Daddy grins, gulps down his tea as if it is makgeolli. "We said we'd never show the pond to any women. But today we'll go!"

Jieun is already jumping and swinging Mila around. Mommy shakes her head, not at the girls but at Daddy and Kyunghwan, singing a song we do not know.

At the pond, my sisters and I pull off shirts and skirts, and run into the water in our panties. Mine are covered in apples, Jieun's in cucumbers, and Mila's in orange pumpkins.

When Kyunghwan sees, he sings, "My face like an apple, how pretty I am, with eyes bright, nose bright, lips bright. My face like a cucumber—"

"No more! Don't sing the next part!" Jieun sprays water at Kyunghwan, but it doesn't reach him. She doesn't like her long face, even though we tell her it's just a song. As we play, the adults bake themselves on boulders, squid laid out to dry.

Mommy wears a real bathing suit. It is black and shiny, with white trim. You can see the roundness of her breasts where the fabric stretches tight. I look down. I have two little nipples but no roundness. Little soybeans no one would want to look at.

"I'm going to catch a great big fish and fry it over a fire!" Daddy yells before jumping off his rock. One arm glued to his side and the good arm in an arch, pointing at the water. He makes a huge splash, and we whistle and whoop. Our voices echo off the rocks.

"Don't forget who won the diving contest every year!" Kyunghwan starts with his back against a tree and runs straight off his boulder. As he falls, he flails around like a panicked animal.

He sinks, screaming.

Mommy shrieks his name.

A silence stretches out in ripples.

"Kyunghwan?" Daddy yells. "Stop it!"

Kyunghwan's head bobs up with a howl. He winks at me.

"He's a Dokkaebi!" I yell.

He fills the pond with a laughter that floats. It is contagious, and soon we are all laughing, holding our stomachs and chucking our heads above the water to stop ourselves from drowning.

"That wasn't funny." Mommy stands above us all, her arms across her chest.

"Oh, come on," Kyunghwan says.

She turns, and Daddy leaves the water to comfort her. Kyunghwan shrugs, gulps air, and goes under.

When everyone is happy again, we cavalry fight. Jieun on Daddy's shoulders, Mila on Mommy's, and me on Kyunghwan's. His hands

push against my butt, nestling me until I am sitting with my legs drap-
ing his chest. His body is slick and I'm worried I'll fall off. He lifts my
arms, flaps them up and down until I feel it—I am high and soaring.

WHEN THE WATER weighs heavy in our bones and it becomes
harder to float, we head to the hills above. Boulders crumble into
pebbles. My skin smells like water and sun.

"This is where we'd fry fish," Daddy whispers. He is so calm
and peaceful, carrying sleepy Mila on his back. There is no fire
pit anymore, but he describes one until I can almost see it: the logs
burning and the fish skin crisping in the heat.

"Let's get some wood," Kyunghwan says. He and Daddy leave,
their bodies hulking together into the forest.

We lie down around Mommy. She sings the apple-cucumber-
pumpkin song, squeezing our noses at our parts. Jieun doesn't mind
so much now, and we hum along, rubbing Mila's cheeks as Mommy
sings, "Our funny round pumpkin."

When Daddy and Kyunghwan come back, Mommy leaves us to
sit with them. It is dark now, and Jieun draws a picture of our family into the sky, using the night's stars to trace our crooked elbows
and noses. Mila drools onto my shoulder. I try to stay awake.

On the first evening of Kyunghwan's visit, the adults told stories
when they thought we were asleep. Of the war that split our Korea,
of a president who controls us, and of people who are dead. But
they are quieter tonight. When Daddy goes to pee in the woods,
Kyunghwan sits closer to Mommy. She looks over at me. I want to
hear what they are saying, but their whispers twist together into
streams.

✦

THE NEXT DAY, Daddy is sick. I bring him his tea and he grumbles that his head is wound too tight.

"Come eat with us," I say.

He wasn't in the kitchen to see it, how Kyunghwan and Mommy smiled at each other. But Daddy gulps his tea and pushes the drained cup into my hand.

He leaves the house without saying good morning or goodbye. When he's gone, Kyunghwan turns to me. "Solee, can you do your uncle a favor? Can you watch Jieun and Mila?"

"Where are you going?"

Mommy stares out the window, but there's nothing there.

"Gasan. Haemi wants to collect more of those plants she loves. Can you be the lady of the house, Solee?"

"Can we go hiking tomorrow, just us?"

"Of course." Kyunghwan squeezes my shoulder.

I smile at Mommy but she doesn't see me. She touches my head, glances at the room where Jieun and Mila are still sleeping.

"Are you really going to Gasan?" I ask.

She bends down to me. She is pretty, with big eyes and pale, freckleless skin. "Where do you think I'd be going?"

I don't know, but I know she's lying.

"Don't worry so much." She smiles. "I'll be back soon with an armful of plants for us."

THEY DON'T COME home for dinner. Mila whines because I burn the rice, and Jieun says she wants oxtail soup, not dumplings. I give them two rice cakes and tell them they are brats, smacking my spoon against the table the way Mommy does when we misbehave. They cry, and everything is worse.

I don't know where Daddy is. I want to tell him everything. How Kyunghwan and Mommy have gone to Gasan. How I am supposed to be the only one hiking with Kyunghwan.

"I miss Mommy," Jieun says.

In bed, she asks for the goddess story. Even little Mila sighs happily when I begin.

"One day," I say, "when the world was new, a goddess came down from the heavens. A man found her and fell in love with her beauty. Knees mucky from kneeling in the dirt before her, he asked her for her name. 'Haemi,' she said. The man snatched the name from the air and swallowed it. He wrapped her in a piece of silk, scooped her up, and brought her home. Mommy is truly a goddess from the heavens, and sometimes when she thinks of the sky, she fades away."

"Again," they mumble together. I stroke their heads and tell them the story again.

I fall asleep in the hallway, against Kyunghwan's door. When I wake up, though, I am floating. "And who do I love?" I hear. It is Kyunghwan. He is holding me in his arms.

Mommy laughs. "Go to bed."

I nestle my face farther into his shoulder so she can't see my gloating. He loves me.

"Good night, Haemi."

In the room, when he pulls the blanket over me, I open my eyes. "I love you, Kyunghwan."

His laughter washes me with the sweet smell of alcohol. There has been so much laughing since he's come, no shouting and stomping. He puts his mouth on my nose, just once and too quickly, and leaves.

I'M NOT SURE what's woken me up again. At first I think it is Kyunghwan coming back to me. But then I hear fighting, the deep snarl in Daddy's voice. I try to go back to sleep.

This time it doesn't end the normal way. There are louder yells, a thud. Mommy's high pitch, though now Daddy is silent. It is shameful. Kyunghwan will hear.

I run into the hall to yell at them. *How embarrassing!* I will say. The way Teacher Han does when we get a question wrong in front of the principal. *You are embarrassing yourselves!*

What I see stops me. Mommy walking into Kyunghwan's room, her face smudgy in the shadows. Glancing around like a thief. She closes the door behind her.

I check on Daddy. He lies on his back, his stomach bulging. One hand between his legs and the other clasping a stick he uses against our calves and palms. *How embarrassing!* I want to yell. He doesn't wake when I shove his shoulder.

"Mother is in Kyunghwan's room," I say loudly. I prod him again. He grunts, a mess of noise erupting out of his mouth. "Did you hear me? Wake up!"

The dead-asleep look on his face doesn't change.

I sit cross-legged outside Kyunghwan's door. I think I can hear them. It sounds like she is crying. It sounds so painful that I clutch my stomach. I want her to stop. They whisper each other's names. I imagine they are kissing. That they are naked, with her round breasts and his hairy, musty armpits.

I clutch Kyunghwan's handkerchief, still tied around my neck.

I put it to my face. I kiss it. When I stick my tongue out, it tastes dirty, not like what I imagined.

I AM WEARING my best shorts, light blue with pink stitching. He will hike with me today, and I will tell him again that I love him. I set two cups of tea across from each other and place the kettle in the middle, just the way he does. I try to fold the napkin into a flower, but I give up. A simple square will have to do.

But instead of coming into the kitchen, he is leaving. I see him out the kitchen window.

I rush into the yard. "Where are you going? Aren't we hiking?" I grab at him. He is petting Dokkaebi's nose.

"I have something to do today. Sorry, Miss Solee." He squeezes my hand. His eyes are doing what Mommy's do. She has infected him. "I have to go."

He is carrying his bag. He is heading to his motorcycle.

"Hiking tomorrow?"

He shakes his head.

"Are you mad at me?"

Kyunghwan unties the handkerchief from my neck and I think he's going to take it back, that he *is* angry.

He only wipes my face.

"I don't want you to go."

"I'll try to come back soon, Miss Solee."

"You don't love me," I say.

When he hugs me, I thrust my face to him so he will kiss me, at least this once, but he shifts and pulls a white envelope out of his pocket instead. "Can you give this to Haemi? When Jisoo leaves for work?"

He shoves it into my closed hand.

He doesn't kiss me goodbye.

Dokkaebi walks with him as he pushes his motorcycle all the way to the end of the road. He turns, a little speck waving. A dog thief. A bad man. I don't wave back this time.

Crystal Hana Kim's debut novel, *If You Leave Me*, is forthcoming from William Morrow in 2018. She has received scholarships from the Bread Loaf Writers' Conference, the Kimmel Harding Nelson Center for the Arts, Hedgebrook, and the Bread Loaf Bakeless Camargo Foundation. Her novel was chosen as runner-up in the 2015 James Jones First Novel Fellowship Contest. She holds an MFA from Columbia University and an MS in education from Hunter College.

EDITOR'S NOTE

When Grace Oluseyi's "A Modern Marriage" came in as an unsolicited submission, its coolness was what first struck us: understated, unfussy, with a psychological core that burns like ice. The story's protagonist, Anu, is afflicted with the self-awareness of those who suspect themselves to be always and uncharitably scrutinized. Her heightened introspection arises from her belief that she is ugly and slow-witted, but the reader suspects that the object of her affection, James, is similarly stricken, if for very different reasons. Head-turningly handsome, a Nigerian immigrant, a black man, bright enough to inspire the jealousy of his peers, he is cognizant of his precarious position in America, an anxiety he expresses as a need to prove others wrong about him. Each character possesses something the other wants. In the hands of a lesser talent, the story could easily have descended into clichéd tropes—of the tensions between first- and second-generation immigrants, of model minorities, of fraudulent green card schemes—but Oluseyi undercuts such stereotypes by keeping the reader's attention fixed on the idiosyncratic dilemmas that face her characters. In particular, the story provokes the reader to wonder, between Anu and James, who is the more canny, and whether the emotionally deceptive still deserve love—for who among us is not, to some degree, numbered among their ranks?

Adam McGee, managing editor
Boston Review

A MODERN MARRIAGE

Grace Oluseyi

WHEN THE PHONE rang the night before Anu's wedding, she was packing the last of her boxes for the move across the bridge to her fiancé's two-bedroom apartment in Astoria. She was happy to leave her dirty little studio in the Bronx. James's hipster enclave in Queens seemed like a veritable castle in comparison. Hardwood floors, original paneling. A prewar building, Gatsby era, he told her. A real piece of history.

She should have had the line disconnected days ago but had kept it for the international calls she could not make on her mobile. "Hello?"

"Anu, my darling? *Bawo ni?*" If the soft, accented voice hadn't given it away, the crackling on the line certainly would have. Her cousin Tobi was in Nigeria and was not able to come for her wedding, but she had been calling Anu all week, teasing her about the wedding night and advising her on creams and lotions that would make her skin soft and supple and asking her about her bridal finery, the woven red and gold *aso oke* wrapper and blouse from Lagos that she would wear for her reception. Tobi was excited about this marriage. She had been praying for years for her cousin to meet someone.

"I am fine," Anu replied, and sat on a sealed box.

183

"James?"

"Out with the bachelors." They were going, James told her, to a boxing match in Brooklyn, and then out for drinks. Anu's eyes flickered over the dingy white walls of her apartment. Just in the corner of vision, a cockroach scurried up toward one of the cracks in the ceiling. They normally weren't this bold—perhaps they sensed she was moving out.

"Good." Her cousin sounded relieved. "I have to. . . . I wanted to speak to you, it is very important."

"Oh?" God, Tobi could be dramatic. "Go for it."

"I have not even told your mother, not yet. I—well, I wanted you to know first."

"Are you pregnant?" Anu joked, but when Tobi didn't laugh, she sat up straight. "Tob. You're not—?"

"No—*hei! Olorun maje*," she swore. "No. I'm not."

"Is someone sick?" Or dead? She could see them trying to hide it from her until after the wedding, not wanting to upset her, but Anu always did better when she knew things, saw them coming. "Or—"

"Anu, *jo*, just listen." Tobi inhaled; she was probably smoking, Anu realized. She tended to do that when she was stressed. She pictured her cousin crossing one dark, plump leg over the other, touching her mouth the way she did when she was nervous about something.

Anu was quiet.

"Are you still there?"

"Yes, Tobi."

Tobi's next words came out in a rush, mixing and tumbling over themselves like grains from a bag of rice, landing in no particular order. Anu managed to piece together bits as she went along. James was married. Wife in Lagos. Two children, a boy and a girl, both in primary school. Married six years ago, before he left Nigeria to go to school in New York. It wasn't a state marriage, not really, but he had paid her dowry and taken her from her father's house. . . .

Anu listened. When Tobi was finished, her voice was both high and breathless.

"Anu? *Anu?* I spoke to his uncle this morning, Anu. He was very, very angry. The boy, he said, is just using you for a visa. His own application was denied. Anu!"

Anu hung up the phone.

ALTHOUGH SHE WAS over thirty, badly dressed, too thin, too broad-shouldered, and still possessed the oily, spotted skin of an afflicted teenager, the tall, broad-shouldered PhD student and lecturer James Adeola Adebisi proposed to Anu a scant six weeks after their first date. It was rather exciting.

It wasn't because he was attracted to her. On the contrary, Anu knew that the man found her repulsive. She'd seen the flicker in his dark eyes the day she'd been brought to him by the dean of philosophical studies, who introduced her as the new office assistant and a "fellow West African." The dean had been all enthusiasm: Americans love coincidences, and he milked this particular one for all it was worth. He beamed at the two of them; Anu imagined the corners of his mouth meeting in the back of his head. *She mentioned that she is Nigerian in her interview, isn't that something? Perhaps you come from the same area? Do you speak the same language?*

During the interrogation, Professor Adebisi's face resembled that of a martyr who feels in the eleventh hour that sainthood isn't worth all the trouble. Anu was embarrassed for him, for them. The professor parried the dean's questions with diplomatic skill, greeted her politely, showed her where his keys were, and gave her his office hours. He was dressed in trendy scholar-wear: wool trousers slung low on his hips, corduroy jacket, skinny tie, vintage denim shirt, brown loafers from some obscure Italian cobbler, Ray-Ban glasses, no socks. It made Anu self-conscious about the ill-fitting polyester suit she wore that day, although she didn't own anything better, not really. It cost money, looking so effortlessly casual.

In those brief first minutes, the professor managed to convey through both manner and tone that he hoped their arrangement was temporary, that she would barely see him due to his schedule, and that his life's happiness depended on the joyful hour of her departure. Anu minded little; she understood his position. Being reminded that you are different from your colleagues by the existence of decidedly unglamorous office help is unsettling, at the very least.

"I won't bother you at all," she said with her usual simplicity. He looked startled but didn't respond.

PROFESSOR ADEBISI FIRED off the typical questions during their first day together: *Who are your parents? Were you born here or at home? Do you speak Yoruba?* The answers tumbled from her lips with ease, as she'd answered them many times before, and the answers were nothing extraordinary. Her devout Christian parents were a nurse and a taxi driver. She'd been born in the States, and yes, she spoke a little Yoruba, but understood more than she could speak. In response, he grunted, as if something had been verified.

The professor did not initiate conversation again, and Anu felt foolish when she found herself hoping that he would. He slunk past her every day, mumbling with eyes averted, but his unfriendliness was little deterrent to developing a crush, which she did, and quickly. It was hard not to. He moved with a quiet, old-fashioned elegance that suited him, spent hours listening to music, and lit a candle that filled the office with the smell of cedar and sandalwood long after the other PhD students had retired for the night. His body hunched when he read, as if he were trying to force something out that had lodged between his shoulder blades. Older professors, confident in their tenure, called him brilliant. His peers called him pretentious. Anu found him fascinating.

Anu discovered that he listened to William Alwyn while writing papers and John Coltrane while grading them. She downloaded compositions from both to her Android, drawing odd looks in the subway as she squeezed her face, trying to follow the rises and falls of the strings, harps, and horns. When he ordered sushi from a restaurant with an unpronounceable name that delivered in an elegantly folded box cooled by dry ice, she rescued the carton from the recycling and went there on a weekend. She spent forty dollars for a seat in the back and struggled for an hour to navigate chunks of rice and raw fish to her lips with those wooden sticks. She checked out books he mentioned on his blog, struggling with phrases like *the bourgeois declaration of the rights of the egoistic individual*, and *dialectical materialism as a heuristic in biology*, and other things that were as indecipherable to her as ancient Aramaic.

They were *his* words, though, and because of that, she read them.

ANU WASN'T SMART. Not in the way Professor Adebisi was, anyway.

She realized this years ago, when her parents started getting letters from her school. Anu, they said, might have a learning disability. They wanted her tested. There were special classes she could take, special books for her to read.

Her mother blamed the devil, blamed evil spirits back in her father's village that had stolen her daughter's intelligence, taken her stars at birth. "They will not label my daughter!" she snapped, and would snap Anu in the face and on the head whenever her report card sported those inevitable D's and, at best, C's. She took her for prayer once a week at Faith on Fire Ministries and hovered over her as she struggled with homework until both their eyes were red and darkly circled. Her classmates were oddities, with their cramming and all-night study sessions that somehow left room for sports, boyfriends, and clubs. Anu had church, home, and the gritty little desk under a naked yellow bulb where she propped up her face, elbows aching, as she studied.

Anu graduated high school a year late, accustomed to being a disappointment. *If only she had been beautiful*, she heard her mother sighing on the phone one day to an auntie in Nigeria. *It wouldn't have mattered, then.*

"I READ YOUR blog," Anu told Professor Adebisi one day, after approaching his desk with a stack of books he'd ordered from the library. Kant, Calvin, Hobbes. He stared at her for a moment before moving a stack of papers. She placed the books carefully, soundlessly.

"And?" he asked after a moment, as if trying to decide whether or not her opinion was worth anything. Curiosity won, however, or a need for flattery.

"It was good." She paused. "It's for people like you, though, I think. Intellectuals would like it."

"Huh," was all he said, then asked her to close the door when she left.

The next day, James saw her in the student commons, where she often sat to eat a sandwich while playing games on her phone. He hesitated, coffee in hand; then he came over to her. Anu looked up and immediately lost her appetite. She simply couldn't keep chewing a ham sandwich dripping with mustard and sweet onion sauce when he was sitting across from her, eyes warily scanning her face.

"You shouldn't have said that yesterday," he said. "Not about . . . It's supposed to be for everyone, that blog."

Anu lifted her shoulders in a shrug. Not speaking, she'd learned over the years, was the only certain way of seeming even remotely intelligent.

"If you wouldn't mind . . ." He cleared his throat. "I'd like your eye. On the blog. When I post. Tell me what you think."

"Okay."

"If you're not doing anything after work—food? My last class ends early tonight."

Anu opened her mouth and spoke calmly, like an actress who's spent weeks practicing for a bit part in an enormous production.

"Okay. Thank you."

Surprise flashed across his face, quick as a sleight of hand. "I'm very glad," he said gravely, in that peculiar mix of British and Nigerian accents he'd picked up from years at universities around the globe.

✦

"WHERE DID YOU go to school?" he—James, as she was now permitted to call him—asked her two weeks later.

It was the fourth time they had been out together. Anu wasn't sure whether this meant they were seeing each other. He hadn't tried to touch her or flirt with her, but he looked a little less wary.

Anu paused before speaking. She was feeling particularly confident today, for once. After googling for an hour and a half, she managed to uncover a sushi restaurant in the Village that was dirty enough to seem undiscovered, and the sleeveless linen top she wore actually seemed right for the venue.

"I didn't," she replied. "I—I went to community college for a year."

James nodded. "Too expensive?"

"Yes," Anu agreed, although it wasn't true. Her parents would have been only too glad to fund school for her.

"You can go for free, you know. To our school, since you work full-time." James selected a California roll, ignored the wasabi and soy sauce, and deftly lifted the small bit of cold rice and chopped vegetable to his mouth. "It's our responsibility to make the best of this place, Anu. We're strangers, no matter how many years we're here."

Her stomach tightened, her appetite gone. "My father often says the same thing." She could not tell him about the years of sitting up late, copying her textbook chapters onto small white cards, as if direct replication would make the words more decipherable. He would not understand it, the futile struggle to achieve something that most managed without even trying.

"You don't seem lazy," he observed.

"No," she agreed, and he peered at her over the table.

"Are you angry?"

She shook her head.

"What are you thinking, then?"

"About your sushi," Anu said, and the corner of her mouth curved upward, slightly.

"My sushi."

"Yes." She could hardly make up an impressive truth, so why make it a lie? "I was thinking about my grandmother, back home. And how she would be horrified that we would pay to eat raw fish."

James's face relaxed into a smile, despite himself. He had, Anu noticed, the clearest eyes she'd ever seen. They were as dark as hers, but were so liquid that they caught the light, reflected it, making them seem bottomless. She could look for only a few moments before she had to lower her head. It was too much.

"How Marxist of you," he said, and his voice was dry. He lifted his wineglass in her direction.

"What is that?"

He laughed out loud.

THAT, ANU SUPPOSED, was the moment when they moved to properly dating. He asked her to go to church with him the following week—practically a declaration in some Nigerian circles—and kissed her for the first time one misty evening after classes in the little moss-covered bower where upperclassmen smoked pot during finals week. He warned her beforehand that he was going to do it. She nodded, then held very still. It was pleasant. She was more aware of the warmth of his body than she was of his mouth, which surprised her. Films had led her to expect the opposite.

He pulled back, looked surprised.

"Haven't you been kissed before?"

She looked at him, and his expression was a mixture of shock and—yes, there it was, for the first time—intrigue.

"Jesus."

He made it sound like a virtue. Anu was grateful.

That night he took her to the park to see a play performed in open air. The language was difficult, but she liked the main character. He made eye contact with the audience, tossed roses indiscriminately, grinned at his fellow actors from under a cap of flaming red hair, as if the whole production was based on a joke only they understood.

When she tried to explain this later, he looked at her, that half smile still in place, and shook his head. "You're quite the enigma," he told her afterward. "Ignorant, and shamelessly so, but quite profound."

"Is that bad?"

He laughed. He did this quite a bit when they were together. She was beginning to like it. "We'll see."

Anu looked it up on her phone when he wasn't looking: *enigma*. She liked that. It gave her a reason for her long silences when they were together: She was mysterious, exotic, she told herself. It wasn't that she had nothing to say. She wished he would take her to more things like this. He often wrote of them on his blog—the plays, operas, and films with titles in languages she didn't recognize. It was difficult, James having a life she wasn't invited to join because she lacked the right that cleverness would have given her.

That would change, she told herself. *Enigma.*

"You and *her*?"

Anu was in the department office, out of sight on the floor, where she'd been attempting to trace her computer monitor cord back to its socket. The speaker was Tara Elliot, who had just walked into the office and stopped in front of James's door.

"They told me you and her . . ." She let the sentence dangle suggestively. Tara was a professor in James's department and had been hired two years ago. She was tall, lithe from yoga, and tan from sun, and she questioned everyone in the demanding voice of one who felt that her credentials gave her the right. She claimed to have spent time teaching philosophy in a Gulf country and often mentioned, with smug satisfaction, that textbooks for *her* gender studies classes had been seized and censored by the Ministry of Culture nearly every semester.

There was no sound from James's office. Anu strained to hear. Perhaps, she thought, he was shooting her one of those exquisitely nasty looks he usually reserved for incompetent waiters. Or perhaps his face was blank, a nonverbal indication that she should get out. Or maybe, she thought, throat tightening, he was smiling, nodding, trying to pass off the comment as a joke. He was eager to please Tara. Anu knew this, saw the emails that flew back and forth between them on the office servers, saw how he never disagreed with her on matters of taste, how he puffed up with pride when she praised him. They went to lectures and concerts together sometimes. Tara was an emblem for the part of his life that Anu would never be a part of.

"She's remarkably intelligent," James said of her, for him the highest praise there was. And now—well. Tara was laughing at her, words bursting out between giggles.

"I nearly shit myself when I found out, James. Well, well. She's got a great ass. That video-girl wig has got to go, though."

"Get out," James was saying, and she could barely hear his

next words, although she could make out the fact that—yes, he
was defending her, in sharp, measured words that came together in
phrases such as *you have no right* and *your condescension is rather
common* and *we're all a joke to you, aren't we?*

Anu almost wished he had laughed it off. She stumbled to her
feet, not caring now who saw her, then crashed into a trash can.
Her skin was crawling with the cold-hot prickles that always pre-
ceded throwing up, and she bolted for the hall.

When she emerged from the bathroom, eyes calm but red-
rimmed, James was there, handkerchief in hand. His jaw was set.
She could see bone protruding from under smooth skin.

"She's a fool," he said. His voice was calm with contempt as he
handed her the square of white linen. Anu pressed it to her mouth.
It smelled like him, something woodsy and light.

"Let's go home, Anu."

Anu shook her head, crossed her arms. The stupid weave she'd
installed the week before itched unbearably, like the cheap shiny
wig it was. She'd thought it quite fetching when she did it, forking
over nearly two hundred dollars for it. She thought she had seen a
flicker of something in James's eyes when he saw her that Monday,
but now she knew. *Video girl?* Oh, God.

"People might see," she said by way of explanation, and his eyes
hardened.

"I don't care."

That night in her tiny apartment, she cried in front of him for
the first time. He held her wrists, forced her to look at him, spoke
soft desperate words that poured out quickly. It was the first time
he'd spoken to her in Yoruba since they met. His words were tender
and musical in a way that English simply could not be for him. Her
sobs quieted and he whispered, *"Pele, pele,* I am sorry," over and

over again, kissed her temple, stroked the long silky strands that the hairdresser had so carefully set.

Don't pity me, she wanted to whisper, but he kissed her then, with an intensity that made her ache. His warm hands had slid beneath her clothing to touch her bare skin, splaying over her waist and back. She was overwhelmed by his closeness and could not speak. When she finally did, it was a husky *please* as she shifted her hips toward him. But he pulled away from her, shook his head. There was shame on his face.

Not until they married, he said, cupping her face in his hands, and he held her close to him until she slept.

HE MUST HAVE been really desperate, Anu thought now, resting her aching head in her hands. Not as desperate as she'd been, though. He hadn't defended her to Tara. Not even close. He'd merely stated the facts. He'd been angry. No one wants to be accused of screwing the ugly girl, after all.

The boy, he said, is just using you!

After a few moments of sitting very still, Anu took the phone, dialed out. The call would use up the last of her precious international minutes, but she didn't care. She would be using James's from now on.

Tobi was relieved when she picked up. "Anu—thank God, I was worried. Are you all right?"

"Tobi," Anu said, and her voice was very calm. "I have to tell you something."

She was astonished by how easily the lie slid out. She knew about his wife, she said. He would be divorcing her in a few months, but there were some logistics that were holding up the process. He'd obtained a green card already, but was keeping it quiet. His visa had nothing to do with her. She thanked Tobi for her concern, but she was fine, really. She knew what she was doing.

"Anyway," she finished. "Even if he was, Tobi. Why would you stay Nigerian if you had a chance not to? It's a useless country now."

"You cannot possibly think this is what God wants for you!"

Anu laughed hollowly and hung up the phone again, this time yanking the cord from the wall and placing the phone in a box. Tobi simply could not understand the way it felt, looking up at the sky from the bottom of a pit you've spent all your energy digging.

ANU AND JAMES were married the next day.

It was so hot that tree leaves wilted and insects buzzed lazily, too tired to sting. The ceremony was one that their people would remember as pleasant, if not extraordinary.

Invitations on Japanese rice paper had been printed at the university shop and sent to one hundred fifty people, listing the starting time as 5 p.m. One hundred eighty-five Nigerian attendees trickled in around 8, joining the few white and Asian guests who hadn't been warned about cultural quirks and had thus been treated to hours of watching the DJ and bridesmaids set up. Sagging and swathed in white and red, the tables groaned under the weight of trays that held seasoned rice, goat meat in red pools of palm oil, and hot pepper soup. Glass plates of sweet fried chin chin and roasted peanuts served as centerpieces. It was incredible, Anu thought. No one had ever made a fuss over her before.

James, resplendent in a sleek black tux, surveyed the chaos with disgust. He'd wanted a quiet ceremony at an upstate chapel that he'd frequented while writing his dissertation, but Anu's parents had overruled him, ecstatic that their only daughter had finally found a husband. He had given in with very bad grace.

"Don't let them pepper the soup too much," he'd instructed Anu. "I'll be inviting people from campus, you know."

The guests listened as the bride's uncle gave the opening toast and prayer, thanking God for the union, praying against spells, family curses, and any other tool of the Evil One that would prevent theirs from being a fruitful marriage. All the *babas* and *mamas* raised a hearty "Amen!" A woman shouted out that they would be blessed with twins; everyone laughed. Then they all ate sticky fufu and okra and bitter-leaf soup and sighed and put their hands on their tummies and ate the great plates of rice with piles of sweet fried plantain, chasing the last grains with their fingers, heading for more in the coolers hidden under the buffet tables.

In faintly grease-stained voices, they gossiped about how God had answered the prayers of the bride and how many degrees the groom had and criticized the bridesmaids' cherry-colored dresses for being too tight and ordered younger girls out of good seats so that they could be closer to the high tables. Then they danced with the bride and groom, spraying bills in the air like feathers, rolling bodies undulating as a single teeming organism. Everyone sang along: *You dey make my heart do yori yori!* Then: *Shay u won no d koko?*

James disliked the music. He told Anu privately that they were all rather silly numbers, beneath his dignity. He would have preferred Motown, jazz piano, '70s African highlife. Still, he drew her close on the dance floor, a smile fixed on his narrow face. The dean, his fat florid face flushed with too much palm wine, kissed them both effusively, bragged about his matchmaking, pointed out his wrapped gift of antique Wedgwood china.

Everyone went home on sore feet and felt partly responsible for making the wedding such a success.

THAT PART HAD been quite easy, Anu thought ruefully, watching the last of their guests trickle out in the small hours as her husband helped her into the back of their private car. She had been watching him all that evening, as if they were characters on a reality show where she already knew the outcome. He spoke fondly about how they met and looked at her now and again with half-hooded eyes that she supposed were meant to denote affection, one hand tucked into hers or wrapped firmly around her waist, nestling her against his side.

It was hard not to feel anything during the ceremony or reception, harder than she thought to look the bishop in the eye and lie, say the vows they'd decided on via email three nights before, copying lines from various websites. He kissed her twice during the reception, for pictures and such. His mouth was warm, soft; she felt the hint of scratchiness about the chin.

She was glad, she realized with the violent thrill of a conquest she had no right to make. She was glad she knew about his wife. It would spare her the pressure of being his ideal.

"Good job," he said into her ear when they were settled in the back of the car that would take her to her new life. She nodded, unable to speak through a sudden pressure in her throat. James fell asleep soon after their departure, lulled by the car's gentle rhythm. The heat radiating off his chest made her drowsy, but she did not sleep. Instead, she watched the driver. He'd opened the windows and it was misting outside, a warm faint imitation of rain. The man sang quietly to himself, free hand dangling out the window. Anu wondered idly if the defogger was broken, or if he enjoyed the coolness of the mist on his fingertips and face after a day trapped in the small, hot prison.

Grace Oluseyi is a writer and a book history scholar who divides her time in work and study between London, New York, and the Middle East.

ABOUT THE JUDGES

MARIE-HELENE BERTINO is the author of the novel *2 a.m. at the Cat's Pajamas* and the story collection *Safe as Houses*. Her work has received the O. Henry Prize, the Pushcart Prize, the Iowa Short Fiction Award, and fellowships from the Center for Fiction and the Sewanee, MacDowell, and Hedgebrook writers colonies. In fall 2017, she will be the Frank O'Connor International Short Story Fellow in Cork, Ireland. She teaches at New York University and in the low-residency MFA program at Institute of American Indian Arts in Santa Fe, and lives in Brooklyn, where she is an editor at large for *Catapult*.

KELLY LINK is the author of the collections *Stranger Things Happen*, *Magic for Beginners*, *Pretty Monsters*, and *Get in Trouble*, which was a finalist for the 2016 Pulitzer Prize for Fiction. She and her husband, Gavin J. Grant, have coedited a number of anthologies, including multiple volumes of *The Year's Best Fantasy and Horror* and, for young adults, *Monstrous Affections*. She is the cofounder of Small Beer Press. Her short stories have been published in *The Magazine of Fantasy and Science Fiction*, *The Best American Short Stories*, and *The O. Henry Prize Stories*. She has received a grant from the National Endowment for the Arts.

NINA McCONIGLEY is the author of the story collection *Cowboys and East Indians*, which won a 2014 PEN Open Book Award. She was born in Singapore and grew up in Wyoming. She holds an MFA in creative writing from the University of Houston, where she was an Inprint Brown Foundation Fellow. She also holds an MA in English from the University of Wyoming and a BA in literature from Saint Olaf College. She currently serves on the board of the Wyoming Arts Council. She teaches at the University of Wyoming.

ABOUT
THE PEN/ROBERT J. DAU
SHORT STORY PRIZE
FOR EMERGING WRITERS

The PEN/Robert J. Dau Short Story Prize for Emerging Writers recognizes twelve fiction writers for a debut short story published in a print or online literary magazine. The annual award was offered for the first time during PEN's 2017 awards cycle.

The twelve winning stories are selected by a committee of three judges. Each writer receives a $2,000 cash prize and is honored at the annual PEN Literary Awards Ceremony in New York City. Every year, Catapult will publish the prize stories in *PEN America Best Debut Short Stories*.

This award is generously supported by the family of the late Robert J. Dau, whose commitment to the literary arts has made him a fitting namesake for this career-launching prize. Mr. Dau was born and raised in Petoskey, a city in northern Michigan in close proximity to Walloon Lake where Ernest Hemingway had spent his summers as a young boy and which serves as the backdrop for Hemingway's *The Torrents of Spring*. Petoskey is also known for being where Hemingway determined that he would commit to becoming a writer. This proximity to literary history ignited the Dau family's interest in promoting emerging voices in fiction and spotlighting the next great American fiction writer.

PEN America and Catapult gratefully acknowledge the following journals, which published debut fiction in 2016 and submitted work for consideration to the inaugural edition of the PEN/ Robert J. Dau Short Story Prize.

1:1000
The Scythe Prize
805 Lit + Art
A Public Space
The Adroit Journal
Aliterate
The Asian American Literary Review
Baltimore Review
Barrelhouse
Bellevue Literary Review
Bennington Review
Black Candies
Blackbird
Boston Review
Boulevard
The Caribbean Writer
Carve Magazine
Catamaran Literary Reader
Chicago Literati
Chicago Quarterly Review
Cleaver Magazine
Commentary
The Common
Conjunctions
Consequence Magazine

Cosmic Roots and Eldritch Shores
Ellery Queen's Mystery Magazine
Epiphany
Exposition Review
The Flash Fiction Press
F(r)iction
Fence
Fields
Fifth Wednesday Journal
Four Way Review
The Gettysburg Review
Glimmer Train
The Gravity of the Thing
Great Jones Street
Harvard Review
The Healing Muse
Hyphen
The Iowa Review
Isthmus
Joyland
Juked
Kaaterskill Basin Literary Journal
Kelsey Review
Kenyon Review
Kweli
LA Fiction Anthology
Little Fiction | Big Truths
Louisiana Literature
The Maine Review
The Malahat Review

The Massachusetts Review
The Masters Review
The Missouri Review
The Moth
New England Review
New Ohio Review
New South
Newtown Literary
NOON
North American Review
North Dakota Quarterly
One Story
One Teen Story
The Paris Review
Philadelphia Stories
Ploughshares
Prime Number Magazine
Pulse: The Literary Magazine of Lamar University
Queen Mob's Tea House
The Rumpus
The Seventh Wave
Slice
SmokeLong Quarterly
The Southampton Review
The Southern Review
Southwest Review
sPARKLE & bLINK
STORGY
Subtropics
The Summerset Review

The Sun

Sycamore Review

The Threepenny Review

The Tishman Review

The Toast

Tin House

Tupelo Quarterly

Waccamaw

Washington Square Review

The White Review

ZYZZYVA

PERMISSIONS

PEN America stands at the intersection of literature and human rights to protect open expression in the United States and world-wide. The organization champions the freedom to write, recognizing the power of the word to transform the world. Its mission is to unite writers and their allies to celebrate creative expression and defend the liberties that make it possible.

pen.org